THE PLIGHT OF RONGSENG

MANGAL SING KRO

Made with ♥ on the Notion Press Platform
www.notionpress.com

to my beloved wife

Contents

Preface *vii*

Acknowledgements *ix*

1. The Chained Dog 1
2. The Plight Of Rongseng 9
3. The Lines 15
4. Lives In A River Bank 23
5. A Vegetable Seller 39
6. An Invisible Grass 45
7. A Shadow Behind A Friend 58
8. A Girl Behind A Curtain 67
9. Under A Rusted Tin Roof 76
10. A Dunkard's Wife 86

Preface

Writing and publishing an English book was beyond my dreams. Being from a vernacular, Assamese, medium background I struggled a lot even to write a short and simple sentence in English. A deep passion for learning the English language has led me to write this book. My first book, "Behind the Thirsty Instinct," is a collection of poems. "The Plight of Rongseng" is my second book published by the Notion Press. It is a small bunch of ten short stories (fiction). Each of the stories tries to bring a unique piece for the readers. I thank the Notion Press for giving me a platform to pen down my thoughts through different stories.

Mangal Sing Kro
North Lakhimpur, 2024

Acknowledgements

Reading books has inspired me to press the buttons on my laptop's keyboard to get this output. I thank the authors of different books and journals, my family and well-wishers. I thank Mr Babyson Terang for designing the cover page. I also thank the Notion Press for publishing this book.

Author

CHAPTER ONE

The Chained Dog

The cheerful blinking stars seemed to hide themselves under the black shawls. They seemed to distance away from the crowded Khanapara bus stand. The moon which led the stars in the sky was also wrapping herself with those black shawls. Slowly the sky seemed to cover itself with a thick black blanket after a while. I had been waiting for a bus at the Khanapara bus stand since 8 p.m. along with other people who were also waiting for their buses. Now, it was 9 p.m. and still standing to catch my bus. The thirsty weather started to drink raindrops. At that crowded place, some people were smoking, some were sipping hot steaming red and milk tea, and some were having *momos* with hot and spicy soups. The packets of chips and *bhujia* hanging in the shops were waving with the flow of the winds. Some people hanging bags on their backs and some were holding trolleys in their hands. I was standing, hanging my sky bag on my back and inhaling the smoke of cigarettes coming out from the mouths of my surroundings. A young man wearing a white t-shirt and loose light blue jeans was chewing and spitting gutkha in front of me. I had seen many people chewing gutkha and betel nuts in their mouths. The mixed smell of cigarettes and gutkha along with the smell of urines came out from the nearby area and entered through my two nostrils. The wine shops were as if looking at us to give us a pack of addiction liquid to mould us forever.

After a while, our bus arrived. I stepped up on the bus and sat on the booked seat. When I travel by bus, I always look for the window seat. That day also, I booked the window seat. Surprisingly, a co-passenger sitting beside me was well-known to me, Kanak. He held a puppy on his lap, cast his smile and asked me to sit beside him. I exchanged my smile and thanked him. I opened the window to let the outside wind enter and kiss my face. I felt relieved from tiredness and the pain in my legs due to standing at the bus stand.

"Where did you come here?" He asked me.

"Sixmile," I replied.

"For any important work?"

“My uncle stays at Sixmile. He has been suffering from Dengue, so I come to see him in the hospital.”

The sound of the bus didn’t stop yet. The conductor of the bus was looking for the passengers of Lakhimpur and Dhemaji. He was shouting ‘Lakhimpur- Dhemaji, Lakhimpur-Dhemaji at some intervals. The clock was approaching 9:45 p.m., and the driver slowly loosened his leg on the clutch and pushed his leg on the accelerator to roll the wheels of the bus. I pressed the seat’s lever and pushed the seat backwards, leaned and closed my eyes for a nap. When the bus was swaying on the wavy road amidst the hills of Jorabat, I was just closing my eyes to enter the gateway of sleep. Probably, my closing eyes turned into full sleep after leaving Jorabat. I didn’t hear anything while the bus was roaring on the road to speed up its wheels. It was midnight, the bus stopped its engine in front of a hotel in Amoni. Kanak woke me up to have tea. Slowly I opened my closed eyes, stood up and moved along with him towards the hotel. We had scalding hot milk tea along with mouth-watering *rasgulla*. However, amidst our conversation, he went to buy a packet of biscuits from the nearby shop and fed the puppy. The puppy was tied with a strong iron chain. He looked cute but seemed unhappy somewhere inside. Probably, he was missing his mother. The tears in his eyes shook me inside. His tears might be for other reasons, but still, I felt as if he was away from his mom at that age.

"Where did you buy this puppy?" I enquired.

"At Ganeshguri." He replied.

"It is so cute." I praised.

He went on feeding him. The puppy, probably, was hungry, hence, he was biting the biscuits in a hurry.

"He seems hungry," I spoke again.

"Maybe." He replied, holding the chain in one hand and the biscuit in the other hand.

"Did they allow you to bring it on the bus?" I asked, indicating him towards the conductor.

"They are well known to me." He replied.

Two dogs were walking here and there in front of the hotel. They walked between the buses standing there, perhaps looking for food. They tried to come near us probably feeling jealous of this puppy. They were thin, but had the freedom to roam everywhere they wished. The innocent puppy wanted to go with them, but the chain that was tied around his neck didn't allow him. He barked at them. Maybe, he sent the signal.

A few moments later, the engine of the bus started roaring again. The two headlights illuminated their lights to find the way for the wheels. We, along with other passengers, entered inside and sat on the allotted seats. The driver turned off the inside light and started to roll the steering.

The window was opened and I didn't close it. The dawn's cool breeze was sweeping on my face. The trees standing beside the road were running behind us when our bus left them behind. The green rice plants sleeping at night were startled when the bus engine roared on the road crossing through them. When I arrived at North Lakhimpur town, it was around 6 a.m. The town looked asleep except for a few e-rickshaws waiting for the passengers. A group of dogs was like a gang in the absence of shopkeepers. They seemed to rule and prevent their area.

I came on foot as our rented house was within a walkable distance. One street dog wagging her tail followed me up to our gate. On the other hand, my neighbour's dog tied with an iron chain in the collar was barking at me. He tried to move from his place, running here and there. Probably, he had never seen his society. His loneliness and confining within a boundary perhaps biting into his brain. When we go for a walk and cross the house, that dog always barks at us. Maybe he wants to say something to us, to express his pain. Maybe he wants us to let him flee or to take him outside. I knocked on the door even though a calling bell was available because ringing the calling bell might wake my daughter up.

One day, it was Sunday. The weather was extremely hot. The sun blew its fiery flame from the sky to the earth. So, the wind reduced its flow everywhere to give respect to the sun. As a consequence, we all suffered and took shelter under the shade of the house. The trees of our surroundings themselves were even in trouble as the warm soil grasped their legs. We had a plan to go outside, but we cancelled it. We all rested under ceiling fans to get relief from the hot weather. My wife, Sushi, switched on the television, pressed the button on the remote control, and searched for her favourite channel. Even though she doesn't like to watch any news channels, that day, she watched a news channel for a while. The news anchor shouting on the screen looked like fighting with someone irritated me. That television sound seemed to add fuel to the fire in that skin-burning heat.

"Change the channel. It is better to watch some YouTube channels for real information." I said.

My wife changed the channel and played 90s Bollywood songs.

"As a non-politician, we need unbiased news. Nowadays, it is hard to get such a news channel." I said.

After a while, our landlord rang the calling bell. He took a piece of white paper in his hand. When I opened the door, he gave me that piece of paper and said, "Current bill."

I took it and saw that the amount had increased 3 times more. I felt shocked.

"Per unit price has increased from this month." He said.

I closed the door and lay down on the floor. Sometimes, lying down on the floor gave me a little relief during extremely hot weather. I wanted to sit under the shade of a tree, but there were not any trees on the campus. In my childhood days, we didn't have electricity. We often took a rest under the trees. We looked for a tree with dense leaves. That day, I was dragged to my childhood days.

" It may be raining tomorrow. Today, the weather is too hot." My wife said.

She went inside to the kitchen and brought a water bottle.

"We don't have any vegetables in our kitchen." She said again.

"I don't know how we're going to run our family. Prices of commodities are too high." I replied.

"The conflict between Russia and Ukraine has impacted our economy too.". She said.

" Yes. The European economies are facing a power crisis." I too added the topic. I read an article on war's impact on the world economies in the morning.

"I have seen on Facebook people demonstrating against rising prices."

"What to do, prices are rising all over the world."

In the evening, the weather was boiled by the sun's heat. Our rooms bathed in hot sun heat all day, so, we were sweating even under the ceiling fans. At around 6.30 p.m., I went out to buy vegetables.

I was going on foot towards the market. A dog was wagging her tail and following me. In between the road, the dog met other two dogs and they followed me towards the market. One of them tried to lick my hands as I held a bag in my hand. His steps sometimes interfered with my steps. I tried to walk a little away from him, but wagging his tail, he didn't stop. Two others kept a little distance from me. Sometimes, they went in front of me and sometimes stayed in the back. When we reached the market, they saw other dogs roaming in the market area, so they went back. These types of dogs can feed their stomach by waging their tails when they meet people. At our home, when we take our meal, such dogs often come and sit beside us.

I was looking for fresh vegetables in the daily market. I asked about the prices of different vegetables. Later, I bought roselle, fern leaves and a piece of bottle guard. I avoided eating tomatoes those days because of their burning price. There were often two types of potatoes in the shops; Old potato and new potato. I often bought old potatoes as they were much cheaper than new potatoes. In summer, new potatoes were brought from the hills state, especially from Meghalaya. The sellers called them "*Shillongia Alo* (Potato of Shillong)." One kind of small potato was often also available in the vegetable shops. It is called "*Axomiya Alo* (Potato of Assamese). They were costlier than the bigger size potatoes. So, we hardly bought this potato in the off-season. I heard someone calling my name from my backside when I was ready to come back home. I thought it was someone calling someone else, so I didn't turn back. He called me again, then I turned back. He was my university classmate, Rahan. He was working as a clerk in a government office. I didn't know in which department he worked. He walked toward me.

"My son's name is also Arun." A seller from where I bought vegetables said, after hearing my name from Rahan.

"Hmmm...". I smiled.

"Where are you staying?" Rahan asked me.

"This side." I pointed my finger. I didn't tell him the name of the village.

"Your family..." He asked.

"They are staying with me."

After talking for a few minutes, he departed away.

In the evening around 8' O clock, the lightning and thunder threatened everyone living under the umbrella of the sky. The frogs which often enjoy croaking at night were silent. The fireflies which always give away their lights in the night hid themselves in hidden corners. The rain angrily ran down from the sky and hit the earth. The cool wind swirled and danced with the falling raindrops. I could feel the cool wind wafting into our rooms through the ventilation. The street dogs perhaps looked for a place where they could protect themselves from the angry rain. Some dogs who entered the people's houses were probably kicked back out onto the street. They probably starved, drenched in the rain and spent sleepless nights. The orphan puppies probably were frightened under the lightning, cracking and rumbling sky. They might be crying and looking for their parents.

CHAPTER TWO

The Plight of Rongseng

The good news spread throughout the Rongseng village that day. Most of the villagers felt proud of Jirsong. His father, Jakong, arranged a goat and invited some of his relatives to a celebratory dinner. It was the proudest moment for Jakong and Katu. Some villagers came to congratulate Jirsong on his matriculation result. Many of them encouraged him to pursue for doctor. Jirsong passed the examination with a thirty-six per cent mark. He was the first person who cleared the matriculation examination from Rongseng village. The school was situated around six kilometres away from their village. That year, two students had cleared the examination from Sintu High English School, which was a great relief for the teachers. Because last two years, the school didn't have any passed out students.

In the evening, Jakong and his neighbour Borsing slaughtered the goat and made everything ready to cook. They dug out the earth in the yard and made a fire pit there. The darkness was falling and spreading, so some of the invited relatives already arrived at their house. They were asked to sit on the bamboo mats placed on the floor in the kitchen. Katu brought betel nuts and betel leaves, sat beside them, and offered them to eat.

That night, a total of twenty guests, came to their home, most of whom were relatives. Jirsong's two uncles, Langtuk and Archok, went to help his father. The women, sitting on the bamboo mats, chewed betel nuts, staining their mouths red. A woman spat the red liquid into a corner of the kitchen. The kitchen was a kutcha and thatched-roofed. It had a single door and a window. Two firepits were made in a corner and an earthen pitcher was kept on a wooden stool right beside them. The pitcher was used to hold rice. Katu felt angry when she saw the woman spit inside the kitchen, but she controlled herself. Katu lit up a kerosene lamp and placed it in the centre. Jakong and his friend started cooking both rice and mutton in two fire pits. Jirsong, on the other hand, just sat on a chair beside them. Archok held a kerosene lamp and tried to provide light with it.

The waxing gibbous moon also sprinkled its light, the cloud, however, frequently obscured the light, so, they tried to light up the area with a kerosene lamp. The surrounding was flickered by fireflies as well. A few moments later, the smell of mutton curry started to waft through the air.

" Go and get *horlang* (Karbi's traditional alcoholic drink)," Jakong entered the kitchen and spoke.

Katu went inside a store room and brought a gallon of *horlang*. She also brought a few bell metal bowls and placed them beside the gallon.

Jakong gently ladled the curry, took a piece of mutton and let Archok taste.

"Oh, Yummy!" Archok expressed.

"Langtuk, you go and arrange the bowls," Jakong said.

Langtuk went to the kitchen and asked everyone to sit properly; he poured the *horlang* into the bowls and handed them over to whoever wished to drink. Jakong asked Katu to bring banana leaves which were cut and washed in the evening. He distributed the pieces of banana leaves to everyone sitting there and served the mutton on them. A little later, they dug into the delicious feast, savouring the sweet horlang and enjoying the tender mutton served on banana leaves.

"I haven't seen Arlong these days. Has he gone somewhere?" Katu asked Kabin.

"He went hunting in the jungle. It is already three days; he hasn't arrived yet." She replied.

Arlong was Jakong's brother. He made a gun himself and often went to the jungle for hunting. Sometimes, he brought *dhuna* from the jungle and sold them in the market. Everyone in the village called him the Sikari. Even though Arlong was younger than Jakong, he married earlier than him and looked older as well. He rarely took baths, sometimes once or twice a month, and often wore shabby grey clothes, making stains less noticeable. He lived alone in the deep jungle when he went hunting. His right calf was misshapen by a bear attack. The bear had eaten some of the flesh, so his right leg looked like a fleshless calf. He still didn't stop hunting.

While everyone was having dinner, they heard the loud exhaust sound of a motorcycle. They all knew it was Langbi. He studied up to class seven and could barely read English. However, he had learned how to give injections and administer saline. When villagers fell ill, they called Langbi, as he was the only person who could give medicine, injections, and saline. They were reluctant to take sick people to the hospital because it was almost 40 kilometres away from the Rongseng village. The roads were also unpaved. To catch the bus, they had to arrive at 6 a.m. at the bus stand. Additionally, most of the villagers didn't speak Assamese, the common language in the region.

"Langbi is coming; probably someone is sick," Kabin said.

"A boy of this house has been suffering from fever. I heard he is trembling in cold and vomited frequently." -Katu pointed her finger to a house and said.

"Last week Bitung also passed away from such fever," Kabin added.

"Yesterday, Langbi said it is malaria and typhoid," Katu said.

"Why are you both talking about diseases during eating? Give me that *kerahi*" Archok asked Katu.

Katu took the kerahi and gave it to Archok.

Archok again served the mutton to everyone.

They all finished their dinner and sat around two kerosene lamps. A single kerosene lamp couldn't provide enough light; therefore, they lit up one more kerosene lamp. The time was around 8 p.m. then. All of them chewed betel nut in their mouths except three children sitting there. Langbi probably heard the news of Jirsong, hence he came on foot to their home.

"Please come to this site and be seated here." Jakong welcomed him and offered a wooden stool.

" It's ok. I heard the news of your child. It is good news for our village." He appreciated.

"Yes, fortunately," Katu replied.

"Whatever. It is a great news for us. Oh, one thing, we all should buy mosquito nets. This malaria fever occurs from the biting of mosquito." He addressed everyone sitting there.

"We have just finished our dinner." Jakong tried to say something to Langbi.

"It's ok. I just have tea there." He pointed to a house where he went to check the fever of a boy.

"Please have betel nut." Katu offered betel nut to him.

Tobacco and slaked lime were also available in the betel nut case. Langbi, mincing tobacco on his palm, said, "I am spreading awareness on this disease."

"It is a good work. We should be aware," Jakong replied.

He also talked with other people seated nearby. However, after talking for around twenty minutes, he left. A little later, the loud exhaust sound of his motorcycle echoed through the village, announcing his departure. Langbi's house was near the bus stand. He was about 45 years old, but still a bachelor. Wherever he went, people recognized him. Because the roar of his motorcycle signalled his presence.

It was eight thirty in the evening, but for the villagers, it was like midnight. Kerosene lamps and torchlights were only the sources of light in the vast darkness. The guests also left for their homes.

The next morning, Jakong woke up, untied the bullocks from the shed and then headed to the farmland to plough. Katu started washing the utensils which were used at night during the party. Their daughter, Kajir, also woke up and came outside the room.

"Is my brother still sleeping?" Kajir asked.

"Go see if he's awake," Katu replied.

"*Oh ik, oh ik* (brother, brother), wake up, wake up." She knocked on the door.

Jirsong was still under a warm blanket and felt cold and trembling. He stood up, wrapped himself with a warm blanket and then opened the door.

"*Oh Pei* (mother), brother is suffering from fever," Kajir called her mom.

Katu came fast and saw her son was trembling in the cold. She touched her palm on his forehead.

"It is very warm!" She exclaimed.

She brought one more blanket from their room and handed it over to him.

"Go and sleep well. Cover up your body properly with this blanket." She said.

She was afraid of the disease. Some people in the Rongseng village had already died from malaria. She went to Langbi's house, described her son's condition and came back.

Thirty minutes later, the roaring sound of Langbi's motorcycle was heard and the sound became louder and louder while he was approaching. He arrived a few minutes later to check up Jirsong.

"I am giving you some tablets and let him eat after the meal. But it will be better if you take him to the hospital as early as possible." He said after giving an injection.

He showed the bill and left the place.

Katu felt helpless in that moment. Thousands of questions ran through her mind. She thought what amount of money would it cost? how would they take him to the hospital? how would they communicate with the doctors and nurses? etc. etc.

CHAPTER THREE

The Lines

The Lankthing River flowed slowly through the Angkung village and poured into the Langbi River. Different species of fish moved freely and played under this silently flowing water. The turtles always flipped and flew amidst the fishes and the frogs often stayed on the bank to look for insects. When the water hyacinth bloomed on both sides of the river, they seemed to swallow the blue water. Thousands of white herons walked and searched fishes in the river every day. Kingfishers came to hunt in the river when they felt hungry. They often flew along the river and kept their eyes on the flipping fishes.

All the houses in the Angkung village were thatched-roofed *Hemthengsong* (stilt house). Every household had a *Hemtap* (tree house). The *Hemtaps* were made especially to protect themselves from elephants. When elephants entered the village, especially at night, the parents took their children up to the *Hemtaps*. The people lived in harmony and their households were thinly scattered in the area. Different trees shadowing the surroundings were sheltering thousands of birds and animals. Sometimes, the birds appeared like black clouds when they flocked and flew together in the sky. The people especially youths of the village organised the *Ajir* (community network).

Sowing and harvesting seasons of rice were the peak seasons of *Ajir*. Every year, during the harvesting of rice, men took part in *Hacha Kekan* at night. Women arranged *Hor* (rice beer) for the dancers. The harvesting seasons always seemed like festivals.

The villagers went to do Jhum cultivation by crossing the Lankthing River. In summer, the water level often rose high as the clouds often poured rain down to the earth. So, the villagers use boats to cross that river. The village head, *Kangbura*, often arranged meetings to discuss different issues of the village. A couple, Sarkang and Kabon, lived in that village and had two sons, Longki and Thengtom. Their house had a *Hemthengsong* and a *Hemtap*. The *Hemthengsong* was made below the *Hemtap* and was partitioned into three rooms. One room was a kitchen where a *Batlang* (Dryer, used to dry fish and meats) was made just above the firepit. They had always kept a black burnt kettle beside the firepit to boil black tea. They also kept bottle-guard shells in the kitchen beside the *Batlang* from which they used to cook *Barasurja* (Steam sticky rice). When the winter came and blew the cool waves, they all often sat beside the fire in the morning and evening to warm their cool bodies.

One day in summer, Longki, who was around 14 years old went to a deep and eerie forest with his friends. The sun had thrown its hot rays from the sky, but still couldn't warm the cool forest. The appearance and sounds of red junglefowl sometimes puzzled Longki, making him wonder whether they were domestic or forest birds. He felt shocked when monkeys leapt between the trees in the deep silence. The Lanklok River flowed through the forest like a giant snake slithering through the trees. Longki and his friends decided to take a refreshing dip in the river.

Unfortunately, the next day, Longki fell ill which caused his parents to tense. His 12-year-old brother Thengtom went out to look after their cattle. In summer, he often put off his shirt and pant, held them in his right hand, gripped his left hand at the tail of an ox and crossed the deep Lankthing river. When he crossed the river by holding the tail of an ox, he felt like flying in the vast blue sky like the soaring birds. At the grazing land, he met other boys who were looking after their cattle. They mixed up their cattle and let them graze together. The boys always took dried chestnut leaves with them when they went to look after the cattle. They plucked raw cannabis leaves, chopped them into micro-pieces and let them dry in the sun rays. When they became dry, they were rolled with the chestnut leaves to make a *Beedi* and then smoked.

Longki had been ill for 3 days. His body temperature was soaring high. So, his mom went to the oracle.

"Is *Phu* (grandfather) there at home?" She asked, standing in the yard.

A girl came out, rolled her eyes and said, "Yes, he is. Come inside."

Phu was sitting on the *Inghoi* (traditional wooden stool) and drinking salted red tea in a huge bell metal bowl.

"What happened?" He asked.

" Kardom (greeting) Phu" She shook her hands without touching his (Karbis' traditional way of greetings). "Longki has been ill for three days. I come here to ask you for this?" She stated.

"Has he gone somewhere before his illness?" The oracle asked.

She described everything about where Longki had gone, what he had done etc.

A few moments later, the oracle brought something in his hand, sat on an *Inghoi*, chanted mantras for a few minutes and said, "You have to sacrifice a cock for the river where he took a bath."

After talking for a few minutes with the oracle, she left the place.

They arranged everything and performed the sacrifice one day later. Fortunately, Longki recovered from his illness the next day.

The people of the Angkung village slept early in the evening and woke up early in the morning. Every household reared poultry. In the morning, the crowing of cocks from every household seemed like playing different music. When the lights began to scatter in the sky, the density of crowing of cocks began to rise.

One night, at around 2 O'clock in winter, Kadom suddenly woke up, because the weather was freezing her that night.

"*Voh ku ethe lo* (first round of crowing)," She said, trying to wake Sarkang up.

Sarkang didn't reply even a word. He was in deep sleep. Kadom got up and lit the fire in the firepit. She kept a water-filled black burnt kettle beside the fire and then sat on the *inghoi*. At around 4 a.m., when all the roosters of the village exchanged their crows, she started making *hor* (rice beer). She prepared *hor* to observe their annual ritual. Because the ritual needed *hor*. In winter, every household observed their annual rituals.

The villagers went to the market on foot. They had to cross vast, deep and silent forests to reach the market. When the heavy rains and the storms blocked their way, still they pressed on, getting drenched along the way to get the essentials they needed. If they left for the market at

4 a.m., they usually didn't get back home until around 11 p.m. So, when the darkness erased the light in the evening, the torch lights were only the sources of light to lead them home. The Lankthing River seemed to show them the way when everyone and everything slept silently at night. The villagers always followed the river to reach the market and then to return home. They mostly went to the market to buy salt. Sarkang brought a radio from the market one day. When he played songs and let the sound waves flow in the air to reach up to the ears of the villagers, they thronged to see that radio. He often played the radio while he worked on his farmland. Two weeks later his neighbour also brought a radio. He always turned the volume high in intended to compete with Sarkang.

Ten years later, there was a conflict between two religions. The root of the conflict originated from the personal fight between Longki and Mindar. Mindar, about 20 years old, was a relative of Kangbura.

Kabin wrapped her two-year-old daughter Mirdan on her back with a *Piba* (traditional baby carrier) and went to the *Ok Kipru* (traditional fishing) at Lankthing River. Some people were shouting against each other's religion even at the *Ok Kipru*. The *Ok Kipru* area became crowded. Some people were completely drenched and others were half-wet. Women held *Ingkrung* in their hands to catch the fish and tied the *Burup* around their waists. The organisers sprayed water on the people who tried to cross them to catch the fish.

The beauty of the Lankthing River was lost over time. The *Ok Kipru* culture of Angkung village destroyed the river's rich ecosystem. Once a place of reverence, it had become their main fishing ground. The fishes always swam in fear. The frequent *Ok Kipru* had led to the extinction of different fish species from the river. The long-necked herons were not always seen hunting for fishes. Their populations had declined significantly. Once the water, which had looked blue, turned into brown. The decorative water hyacinths rarely bloomed on both sides of the river now. The density of the birds' chirping and twittering sounds also diminished. The sounds of shouting, screaming and crying, especially at night, often entered Kabin's earholes instead of the soothing sound of the river's flows. The people of Angkung village were now divided in the name of religious beliefs. They tightened the rules of marriages between the religions. The innocent Mirdan still didn't know who her grandparents were. The embracement of religion by her parents before her coming into this world had made a strong barrier between her home and her grandparents' home.

One day, after harvesting rice, Sarkang arranged a dinner party at home. Except for his elder son, Longki, he invited all his relatives. He arranged a medium-sized pig for dinner.

"Longki hasn't visited our home since his marriage. Mirdan is now two years old. She still doesn't know who her grandparents are. Shall I invite them to our home?" Kabon unable to hold back her emotions, tried to request Sarkang.

"Don't take his name again." He scolded her.

"He is our son. Look at Mirdan, how cute she is."

" The person who doesn't want to eat even food in our home. Is he, our son?"

Kabon helplessly left the topic and went inside the *hemthengsong*.

"He was raised here, in our religion. He shouldn't behave like this." Thengtom who was sitting beside them said after her mom left the topic.

"I couldn't understand how he became blind." His father stated.

"I heard some people again came to propagate a new religion," Thengtom said.

"It might be the people of your brother's religion."

"No, it was a new religious group."

"Again, our people will be divided."

" What to do? We cannot prevent them." Thengtom expressed.

In the evening, the sun which sprinkled its lights all day long started to hide itself below the horizon. The mynas and herons who had gone hunting in different places started to take a rest on the nearby bamboo bushes. The darkness started to swallow the evening's golden lights and tried to rule over the night. A couple of owls who often came to the mango tree near their house to sleep during the days stayed awake. Probably they would go to hunt different insects at night.

They stopped the discussion and waited for the guests.

At night, foxes howled near the forest. Their sounds travelled through the air and spread throughout the village. The buzzing sounds of insects at night also filled the air like music in the silence of Angkung village, as no one screamed and cried that night. However, sounds from Sarkang's house could be heard up to some extent, as a dinner party was being hosted there. When everyone was eating busy and chewing yummy pork boiled with sesame seeds, one of their relatives, Longbui who arrived late for the dinner party, said, "I heard our village will be divided into two parts. One part will be under another state. The Lankthing River will be the boundary. People living in the forest side would get special facilities."

"Who will divide our village?" Sarkang asked.
"The government," Longbui answered.

CHAPTER FOUR

Lives in a River Bank

A five-year-old boy was playing with an innocent baby dog on the verandah of their newly constructed house. The house was constructed under a government scheme. The innocent boy sitting and lying on the floor had derived immense pleasure as it was his first experience on such a plastered floor. The day was sunny; the dusty wind was slapping his face as full-loaded trucks were running in between on the nearby dusty road. He still didn't care about them. His elder sister studying in class 3 was playing with the children of her age in the backyard of the house. The Barkang River was silently flowing on her way to meet the Brahmaputra River. The beauty of the river was destroyed by some people by extracting boulders, stone chips, sand gravels and so on. The noisy sound of the bulldozers, trucks and tractors along the river might raise millions of questions even in the mind of this innocent and playful five-year-old boy. The Barkang River pouring down from Arunachal Pradesh was mesmerizing, especially during winter. The fresh and cool water and the boulders along the river invited thousands of tourists from different parts. People from different places came for a picnic and enjoyed with friends and families. Longki came from his farmland with a plastic bag in his hand. He went early morning to pluck vegetables from his farmland. His eldest daughter, Kajir, had already cooked the breakfast and hence waiting for her father's return. Longki had been protesting against the destruction of natural beauty, but nobody took his protest seriously. When he came across the river, he often felt melancholic over the decaying beauties of the river. He could not admit himself to the college. He left his study after class twelve. He arrived at around 10 O'clock and went for brushing his teeth. They did not have their water well; hence, he went to his neighbour's water well.

"Where is *Po (father)*?" – Kajir came out from the kitchen and asked his brother Monsam.

"Farmland." He said, indicating with his finger and grasping the sleepy baby dog. The dog screamed and left the place.

"Are you feeling hungry?' – Longki asked his eldest daughter after keeping a toothbrush in a brush case.

"Yes, I am, I fed my brother, he was crying." – Kajir said, sweeping the floor.

"Kache, come and have food." – Her father called up his daughter.

Kajir poured water into three glasses and asked her brother to eat.

"No, I will have later."- He answered and came closer to his father.

Longki ran his right-hand fingers on his head and said, "Eat a little, I will buy a new shirt from the market for you."

Longki was thinking about the future of his three children. After Mary left this world, he was bringing them up alone.

It was Monday. Some people from Arunachal Pradesh were coming for the weekly market. The market was around 5 kilometres away from Longki's home. The two

traders were standing near his home as it was the road through which people from different places came for marketing. They brought different organic products from their land to dispose of the surplus in the market. They were waiting to buy at a cheaper price from them. The Barkang River was a stumbling block for them during the summer. The river took a huge shape during the summer. Once the cluster of trees standing on its bank were letting the river flow on her way and protecting the Ronglangso village. But they had been cut and sold out by some people.

A huge sound of a speedily running tractor disturbed their conversation.

"Don't let your *Muso* (little brother) go towards the road." – He expressed his dissatisfaction over the trucks and tractors exploding dust and sound on the dusty road.

"Yes *Po,* he has been playing alone from the morning." – Kache replied.

"Kache, play with *Muso* at home."- Kajir ordered her sister before stopping her reply. She spooned a little rice and curry from the bowl and asked her father to take them.

"No need."- He said.

Monsam stood up and held a small wooden stool in his two hands and bent down, pushing the stool with his right hand as if pushing a toy car. He made a sound like the sound of a car from his mouth.

The condition of the kitchen was very pathetic. The rusted tin roofs and the holes over there were always ready to welcome raindrops inside the room. The white and glittering stars spreading in the sky could even be seen from inside with the naked lens of the eye.

"Why didn't you cover the lid on the water pots?" – Longki asked Kajir, indicating the water pots which were kept on the floor near the backdoor of the kitchen.

"Sorry *Po*, I forgot to cover the lid while I was busy cooking." – Kajir replied.

Kajir was 12 years old then. She often helped her father with different house chores. Sometimes she cooked alone and fed her sister and brother. Her father went to their farmland in the early morning. Hence, she cooked their meal alone. She was often obliged to take leave from the class to take care of her brother.

Longki washed his hands and went to see the young betel nut plants. He checked the fences which were made of bamboo sticks to protect from cows and goats entering the campus. The sticks were becoming dry and hence they could be used as firewood. Some of them were missing. Longki suspected one of his neighbours, Sarthe. Once, he was beaten by some people for an accused of thief. He had a bad record in the past, hence when such activities happened in the village, he had often been suspected. His wife also had such bad habits. When the women of his neighbours flocked together, she became the main topic of their gossip.

The planted betel nut plants were happily growing extracting energy from the dried cow dung which were placed at the bottom of the plants. The drops of the rainwater also made them healthy and raised their height. The green surroundings brought a little happiness to Longki's mind. A tree with huge branches standing beside a betel nut tree invited wild birds to have fruits dangling from its twigs. The chirping birds often flew around the tree.

Longki came back and got ready for the weekly market.

"*Po*, bring *jilepi*."- Kache got up and approached her father.

Monsam wanted to go with his father, hence, he ran toward his father. He started to cry and held onto the carrier of the bicycle.

"*Bong, popo* will bring *jilepi,* come." – Kajir stepped down from the floor and consoled his brother. She embraced him with her arms and asked him not to cry. She rather asked him to wave his hands to say tata to his father.

At around 11.30 a.m., two people sitting inside an auto came to the village and announced their product. They came for an advertisement for a product. Monsam ran towards the road who didn't understand anything about what they were announcing. He rather waved his hands and leaping with joy at their entrance gate. Kajir ran fast towards her brother to get back to him. She held his hands and pulled him towards her.

"Don't go to the roadside *Bong, Phangkedong* (Child lifter) is roaming on the road." – Kajir warned her brother scaring him.

Kache was playing with her friends in the backyard of the house. They were busy making puppet toys from taro plants. Two of them made two human shapes, male and female and celebrated their marriage. Kache and Kadom acted as a seller of goods and her cousin Rupson was a buyer. They sharpened some small sticks of bamboo to use as pillars for the playhouse. The taro leaves were used for roofing sheets for the shop, leaves of jackfruit were used as money and sand as rice. Monsam was also playing with them, but when those people were announcing their product, he ran towards the road.

"Kache, take care of our brother, I am busy washing utensils." –Kajir said and came near the backdoor of the kitchen and washed the utensils.

"*Bong*, come and play with us." –Kache called out to Monsam with a loud voice.

Kajir worked a lot at her age. The children of her age usually didn't do as she did. After the death of her mother, she began to work in the kitchen. The children of her age in the village were taking tuition four days per week besides daily classes in the school. She sat on a small and low wooden stool, humming a *Karbi* song while washing the utensils.

Bunches of white clouds were freely moving in the sky following the way where the winds led. The clouds hid the golden rays of the sun sometimes and unleashed them after crossing the position from where the rays came. Kajir left all utensils in the sunshine which she washed. She came inside her room to take a rest for a while.

"Is anybody there?" – Longsing called out from the outside with a medium tone.

Kajir came out and saw her uncle, Longsing.

"Where is your father?" – He asked.

"My father went to the market, please be seated, uncle." – She brought a plastic chair from the room and let him sit in the verandah.

Longsing came from *Rongman* by bicycle which wasaround six k.m. away from *Ronglangso*. He wore grey colour jeans and a white T-shirt that seemed to be newly bought. The scent of the new clothes still has not vanished from them. He came to meet his girlfriend, Kanchan in Ronglangso whose house was just beside Longki's house. Longsing and Monsam were cousins in relation. Lonsing did visit their home sometimes when he did come to meet his girlfriend. Kajir came out from the kitchen, brought a jug and glass in her hands, placed on the table and asked him to have water.

"I will make tea, uncle." – Kajir said, and went back to the kitchen.

"Ok." - He replied, sitting alone on the verandah, taking out a smartphone from his pocket, tried to open his Facebook account. He looked at the top of the screen; and saw the cross sign instead of the bar. He held the mobile, raised his hand and moved it to find out the bar sign. Kajir came out with a tea cup and biscuits on a tray.

"Please, have red tea uncle." - Kajir said humbly.

Longsing took the teacup in his right hand and two pieces of biscuits in his left hand. The scents of ginger put in the tea filled his nostrils. The puppy shaking his tail came closer to him with the hope of sweetening the hungry mouth. He took out two pieces of biscuits and fed the puppy from one of them. After having tea, he left there.

Longki moved ahead to the crowd after parking his bicycle in the cycle stand beside a *Peepal* tree in the market. He followed the footsteps of others who came to the market. Loud music was playing in a shop, sometimes they kept on announcing their products in a microphone. A few faces were known among thousands of unknown moving faces in the crowd. He turned left from a straight way, entered the second-hand market, and bought a shirt and pent for Monsam. He went towards a *jilepi* shop. Some people were thronging in front of the shop, asking for Jilepi. Longki took out twenty rupees from his purse and handed over it to the shopkeeper in exchange for a half kg of Jilepi.

Longki held a plastic bag and went towards the vegetable market to ask the market prices of brinjals, chillies and ladies' fingers. He produced these vegetables in his small farmland which he used to sell in the village's grocery shop. He did not have land for cultivation, so, he used to cultivate in the bank of Barkang River. He saw his relative aunty of *Terang Arong* (Terang Village)selling vegetables. She used to eat slaked lime and tobacco with betel nut and betel leaves. Her lips were wearing red liquid of the chewing betel nut and her black teeth were gleaming when she parted her lips.

"This year Aunty has been reckoning up notes...." Longki tried teasing her.

"No, just cultivated small area." She chuckled.

"Please have betel nut." She offered a small beg where she used to keep betel nuts.

The sun rays licked on the brinjals and chillies reducing their freshness. Probably, most of her brinjals and chillies had already sold out. Longki sat beside her and opened the plastic bag that was handed over to him.

The time ticked 1 O'clock. Some people were stepping back from the market. A drunkard around the age of fifty took steps in a swinging way and sang a broken Hindi song. He drank *Sulai* in the market that used to be sold in the west corner of the market. Longki slowly peddled the bicycle and crossed him. A gentle wind was blowing and a swarm of bees was flying following the way the wind heading. Longki felt relaxed after coming out from the busy market. The blowing wind erased the sweat of his body. He stopped on the road and looked towards the flying swarm of bees for a while. He unbuttoned his shirt, folded his pant up to his knees and then paddled his bicycle to let his whole body cool down.

Monsam frequently went to see towards the road to check whether his father was coming or not. Probably he was missing his father; he wanted to sit on his lap and ask lots of questions. He did not know who his mother was. He often asked about his mother. Longki couldn't find the answer whenever he asked such a question. Somehow, he managed to get rid of them.

When Longki arrived home, Monsam ran with joy and happiness towards his father after impatiently long waiting. He grasped the cycle frame, got on and sat down on the front baby seat.

"Po, have you brought *Jilepi*?" Mansam eagerly asked his father. He rang the bell many times and tried to shake the handle. "*Oh Ni*, father has arrived!" he shouted happily.

"*Opo*" Kache called her father with happiness.

Monsam got down and snatched the *Jamborong* (hand-woven bag) hanging from the handle of the cycle. He quickly took out the pieces of *jilepi* and started to eat after giving them away to his two sisters.

A nanny goat was bleating and searching for her kids. She went for grazing and now came back. Her kids were also bleating perhaps they were hungry and waiting for Mother's arrival. They ran towards their mother, folded their legs and sucked the milk joyously. The sun was about to set on the horizon, and the cool wind blew from the riverside, but the bulldozers and trucks were still loading sand gravel in the river. The women who were working in the river were coming back to their homes. Longki went towards the grazing field to untether his two bullocks. He hadn't seen the ropes tying at the horns. They were stolen away by some people. But luckily the bullocks were still grazing in the field. The grazing fields were vanishing day by day as the river brought the sands from the different erosional sides and placed them on the grazing fields. The number of goats and cows in the village had been decreasing because of the lack of such grazing fields. Longki brought his two bullocks from the field and tied them in their shed.

The time reached 7.30 in the evening. The wild birds taking shelter on the tree were flipping their wings and their chirping sounds created a funfair situation. They always came to take shelter on the tree, probably, they felt safe. Here nobody came to wake them up in their deep sleep. Longki warned his neighbours not to kill birds inside his campus. He was cooking dinner in the kitchen. He cooked roselle and lady's finger boil with dry fish and potato *bhaji*. He heard a voice calling from the outside. The sound bursting out from the cooking pot prevented him from recognizing even the familiar voice. The smoke that came out from the firewood also created tears in his eyes. He wiped his tears with his bare left hand and came out to check who it was. He saw Sarsing sitting on the wooden bench on the verandah.

"Oh! Sarsing, I could not recognize your voice inside from the kitchen." – Longki said and sat down on the bench.

"No problem." – Sarsing replied.

A neighbour often used to go to their neighbours' homes without any reason sometimes. Sarsing was Longki's schoolmate and they were still neighbours. Now, he is a high school teacher. They often talk and discuss about society and politics, especially in the evening time. Longki often had the eagerness to know about different situations of the country from Sarsing who often kept updating his knowledge.

"I have seen you in the field. Probably you went out to fetch your bullocks." - Sarsing said leaning his back on the wall.

"Oh yes. Had you gone that side?"

"I was in a hurry and a little distance from you."

"Hmm. You know our grazing lands are disappearing day by day." – Longki expressed.

“What to do, most of the villagers are working in the river. We have been raising our voices but it is worthless. One day this river will wash away our village or may turn our paddy field into desert." – Sarsing replied.

"True. Some people have even started to dig our village side hence the river is encroaching on our village. Yesterday, I told a few people not to dig the village side. They replied that they were working under the command of the landowner. I was shocked." – Longki said.

“Yes really. People of our society have started to leave from farmland. They are moving from a producer to a consumer society. No doubt they are now earning a little more than earlier, but this is threatening our future and our society. We can’t buy land in other places if this river washes us away." – Sarsing expressed his thought.

"I always think about our childhood, Sarsing. How had spent those days in the clean and clear environment.”

They interchanged their words for a few minutes. The moon started to appear clearly in the sky along with enormous stars. The leaves of the tree standing beside the house prevented the streams of moonlight and shadowed the front of the verandah. The sounds of the flapping wings of bats were heard, perhaps, the bats came for a hand of ripened banana dangling from its tree. The puppy ran here and there and barked at the flying bats under the clear moonlight. Longki wanted to strike a humming mosquito many times but failed. He lit up a cigarette, smoked and let out the smoke to chase away the mosquito. A full load of the truck was roaring, disturbing their conversation, hence, both of them kept silent. But a few minutes later, when the sound became fainter and fainter Longki broke the silence by handing over a teacup to Sarsing.

“Please have tea.” Longki offered.

"I came here after having tea at home," Sarsing replied.

"Have for refreshment."

"Can I have a glass of water before having tea?"

"Sure."

Longki ordered Kajir to bring a glass of fresh water.

"The trucks are transporting even in the night." Longki once again brought back the topic.

"What to do, we don't have the power to stop them. These are used to construct public roads and bridges. In the name of development our places are turning into a desert." – Sarsing replied in a low tone and sipped the tea again. "

"I am thinking about my children. If this river chases us away from this place, where would we go? The government still hasn't done for our protection. We have asked many times to our local MLA for strong protection but he still hasn't provided us." Longki woefully expressed his thoughts once again.

The Borkang River was throwing gentle winds towards the village. The baby goats were happily jumping in the yard enjoying the moonlight. The mother goat was even trying to come out from the shed, pulling the rope that was tied around her neck. The squeaking bats were still flapping their wings around the banana tree. The bullocks under their shed were also waving their tails. Sarsing looked at the ticking clock hanging on the wall and said, "I am leaving. I will go to see your vegetable garden one day."

"Sure, do visit sometime," Longki replied.

Monsam was in a deep sleep under the moving ceiling fan that even the blood sucker-long proboscis mosquitoes failed to wake him up. The bulb beaming the light dangling from the wall was swirling of moths. Longki tried to wake up his son to have dinner. When Kajir heard his father's voice, she came inside and said that he had eaten his dinner already. She tied the mosquito net, went back to the kitchen and arranged for dinner.

The next day in the evening, the nimbostratus clouds were moving ahead to the mountain. A hunter kite was stretching out its wings floating under the moving black clouds. The long-necked herons were rolling their eyes still looking for fishes to fill their hungry stomach. The thick layer of the clouds created a huge tension in Longki's mind. Because the heavy rain might raise the water level of the river which might wash away his farmland. He went to the grazing field to fetch the bullocks that were tied with rope. He pulled out the bamboo sticks where the ropes were tied and let the bullocks come to the shed by themselves. Every year, the river was approaching closer to the village by eroding the soil. People residing near the river always felt scared during the summer. They felt relieved in winter. Ten houses in the village had already been washed away by the river ten years back. But after that, the river diverted her way. Now again, the river changed her way and is approaching the village. The bamboo trees, betel nut trees and the houses floating with the river waves ten years back were frequently floating in Longki's mind. He couldn't stay calm, so he just stood and looked at his farmland. Everyone working outside the home was rushing back to their home. But, Longki was frequently looking towards the mountains from where the river streamed down.

A few minutes later, the rain started dropping down and its density increased and finally, it poured down heavily. He drenched himself in the rushing rain and helplessly looked at the rising water of the river. His wetted white shirt sticking to his body clearly showed his skin. His combed hair fell downside due to the pressure of the falling rain. When the water level grew and the river water started touching his sole, he decided to come back home. The nights fell but the thirsty sky still roaring with drumming rain. The brinjals and chillies plants through which his family filled the rice in their rice bucket plunged into the thirsty floods. The uprooted plants were swirling with the river flows and the insects which took shelter in the branches and leaves of the plants lost with the river waves. The kitchen floor was flooded by the rainwater when Longki arrived home. They could not cook even for their dinner in the kitchen. Kajir, Kache and Monsam stayed inside the room and waited for their father.

"Kajir, Kajir…." Her father called.

"Yes *Po*, we are inside the room." She answered and came out.

The cracking thunderstorms and lightning filled the night. The light streaming from the wick of an oil lamp which kept on the table was flickering. It was only the source of light for that night.

"Bring the lamp this side." He said.

Kajir held around the fuel tank and handed over her father. The soot surrounding the chimney was preventing the light from the wick.

"Are you all hungry?" Longki asked.

"We ate in the evening," Kajir replied.

"*Po*, is the river level rising?" Kache eagerly asked.

"Yes, it is rising."

Longki changed his dress and took a rest on his bed. He joined his hands and kept on the pillow below his head. Thousands of words were playing hide and seek in his head. He closed his eyes and quietly lay down straight parting his legs on the six feet wooden bed. The light of the lightning was reflected from the looking glass hanging on the wall. He could also see the photo of his marriage which was kept on the table even in the night when light flashed inside from lightning. The density of the raindrops decreased after around two hours. The frogs, in the backside of the house, were crooking trying to keep the rhythm with the dropping rain. However, his tension was still gripping his head. His tension was about the rain pouring in the mountains from where the river streamed.

“Kajir, bring the lamp," Longki shouted from the kitchen. “

Kajir came out with a flickering lamp and moved inside the kitchen. Even though the raindrops crossed the roof sheets from different parts and wetted the floor, the firepit was still dry. Because the roof sheet above the firepit was a little better than in other places. Longki arranged the tripod, and firewood and lit up the fire. Kajir also brought dry firewood from the place where it used to be stocked.

Next Morning. After getting up from the bed at around 6 O'clock, Monsam ran towards the backyard to urinate his night-long stock of urine. The grasses on where he always urinated were decomposing. He had been wearing a new shirt and pant from the previous day. Kache sat on the wooden stool on the verandah, her coily hairs were piling on her head as if a bird nesting on it. The rain was drizzling and its intensity to pour down heavily from the dark clouds was still seen. An earthworm was moving wavelike towards the verandah where Kache was sitting.

"Kache, the earthworm is coming towards you. Can’t you see?" Kajir shouted in a rebuking tone. "Go and brush your teeth."

Kajir brought a dustpan that was kept in the corner of the verandah and removed the worm from the place.

“Where is *Popo*?” Monsam asked.

“He went to the river.” She replied lazily.

Monsam's hairs were falling straight down as if they were swallowing his two ears. He was removing booger in his nostrils with his right forefinger. He frequently put out his finger from the nostrils and wiped it out on the hem of his shirt.

"*Bong*, come over here and wash your face," Kajir called his brother.

Monsam got down from the verandah and went to freshen up near his sister. He took out a full mug of water from the bucket and rinsed the water over his face.

Longki stood along with other people who came to see the thirstily flowing river from the mountainside and about to gulp the village lying near the flowing river. The people thronging there murmured about the consequences the villagers would face. His vegetable garden was already submerged in the water. The river reached almost the point where it had left ten years back. The river had already taken away all their paddy field ten years ago, and this time his house was also about to submerge with river waves. The area of their paddy field turned into a company's boulders, sand gravels, and stone chips digging ground. He couldn't claim his land because the company owned it by bidding in the government office. He managed to cultivate in an accretion land, but that year was very unfortunate for him.

CHAPTER FIVE

A Vegetable Seller

A seller always sold leafy vegetables in the corner of Panipur town. His age looked like early 50's. Just beside his vendor was a narrow canal to let the town's dirty water flow out. The canal poured the oily black and dirty water into Dong River. The Dong River flowed through the hills, poured towards the plains, and bypassed the Panipur town. In summer, sewages often blocked the canal and so, the water often overflowed toward his vendor. He always wore unironed black pent and, a blue and grey shirt on alternate days and often wrapped a white *Gamosa* around his neck. His uncombed grey hair that covered up his standing ears seemed to increase his age. In winter, when the cold swallowed the weather, he often wore a black shabby jacket probably bought from a second-hand shop in the town. Nearby his vendor were a few vegetable vendors. Just beside his vendor was a fish-selling shop. Therefore, the rotting fish smell always wafted through the air in the surroundings. Even though he was unknown to me in the beginning, after becoming his regular customer I called him *Khura* (uncle). His name was Dipen. I didn't know his surname. One day, in the evening 6'O clock, when the darkness started to swallow the sunlight and invited the moon to sprinkle its light, a man was bargaining with Dipen

Khura while I was buying fern leave from him. Dipen *Khura* usually sold three bundles for twenty rupees to the customers. But that man asked for five bundles in twenty rupees from him.

“These leaves are available even in the outskirts of this town, why are you taking too much price?" The man said. He was an average height with a bulging belly and wore black colour jeans and a pigeon grey colour blazer above the blue formal shirt. His age looked like early 40’s.

“I have also bought them from others.” – Dipen replied politely.

“You could have been plugged by yourself.” He said again, chewing betel nut in his mouth.

“For how many days can I sell with those ferns growing on the outskirts of this town? I sell every day.” Dipen replied reluctantly. Perhaps his words pricked his head as his facial presentation changed a little.

The man grabbed five bundles, put twenty rupees inside Dipen’s shirt’s pocket, and went away. Dipen called him with a little high tune to show his disagreement, but he didn’t lend his ears towards him. He got inside his blue colour Baleno car and went away from the place thereafter.

“This man always pays less than what everyone pays. Everyone knows his ruth behaviour and one thing do you know he is an officer.” Dipen explained to me after the man left from there.

I read somewhere in economics that a larger bundle gives a higher level of satisfaction. This statement might be true in his case. But, when Dipen Khura wanted to give me an extra bundle, I often rejected his offer. Because I didn’t like to eat fern leaves curry consecutively in two meals. So, I often brought a bundle of ten rupees. The extra bundle would be rotten away as I didn’t have a refrigerator at my home. In my case, that economics theory would be invalid. As a customer even though I looked for cheaper prices often, still I didn't like to bargain with a seller like Dipen *Khura*.

My parents used to produce vegetables, especially taro, brinjal, chilli, etc. and sold them in a weekly market. The weekly market used to be held on Monday. If they cannot dispose of their products in the market, they often sell those items to Siyaram and Jagan who used to come from far away to buy our products.

The people in our village were dependent mainly on rice cultivation. However, they also cultivated taro, brinjal, chilli, ginger, turmeric, etc., in the nearby forest areas. Herds of elephants often came at night to eat rice plants from the rice fields. Some people made *Hemtap* in the rice field to guard them from the elephants. I still remember when my father often went to guard our farmland at night with a torchlight.

The villagers were not aware of the cultivation of cauliflower, cabbage, and tomato which are usually harvested in winter. They were unknown to chemical fertilizers, insecticides, and pesticides. In summer, during the seeding season and sowing paddy seeds, some farmers sang beautiful songs with every step of their ploughing. Everyone carried out their work with the intent of competition. Their family members came to drop off meals for those who ploughed their fields. They ploughed the fields with bullocks. The paddy field turned into a romantic for the newlywed couples. Newlywed brides came to drop the meals for their husbands and ate together in the narrow divider path in the fields.

After around 4 months long waiting, when the people harvested the golden rice and found to decorate the piles of paddy in different shapes in their yards, then they felt relieved as if they got to breathe freely after a long blockage in their nostrils. They felt free as if the tensions creeping on their heads had slipped down on the ground. They felt free as if they could throw heavy things that pushed down their heads. The rich in our village was measured by the amount of rice production. If the piles of paddy in the yard are big, then we said they were rich. In the months between January to February, people often arranged a family picnic.

Siyaram and Jagan came to buy taro, eggplant, chilli, etc. in our village. They came through the muddy road even in the dry winter season as the road never got dry in the entire year. When everyone enjoyed the cool winter and desired for the rain to wet their dusty roads, the hard layer of the road of our village still hid under a thick layer of mud. Therefore, the traders did not like to come to our village.

Siyaram and Jagan were from the same village and they were relatives also. They cycled around 25 kilometres on a non-plastered pebble-scattered road and then came through the *Kutcha* muddy road to reach our village. They could not peddle their bicycle throughout the road. Telephone and mobile phones also were not available in the village, therefore, they made an oral agreement with the sellers in the weekly market to make the goods ready.

The last time I saw Siyaram in the weekly market. He sat beside my father. My father was selling vegetables. I wanted to talk with him as I saw him around 20 years later. I called him *Khura* when I visited my father in the market. He was looking shocked, perhaps he couldn't recognize me. He looked at me confusingly, probably he was unsure whom I was calling. The burning sun above our heads in the sky threw its flames on the ground as it was in the mid-summer. Both my father and Siyaram were sitting under the shade of a plastic tarpaulin roof to protect themselves from scorching sun rays. An ayurvedic medicine shop nearby them had been announcing their products in a mike. Sometimes they kept playing their recorded sounds in high volume. Their sounds seemed to increase the crowd in the market.

"He is my youngest son, Rahul." My father said when I went closer to them.

"*Khura*, how do you do?" I asked him again.

"I am good. Where are you staying now a day?" he asked me back.

"Panipur," I replied.

"What are you doing there?"

"I am working in a private bank."

"Haven't you tried for a government job?"

"No. I am planning to resign even from this job."

"Why? Haven't they paid enough salary?"

"I want to start my own business rather than do it under someone."

As the scorching sun rays were heating the weather, I too sat down beside them under the shade. I heard the sound "ice cream, ice cream, ice cream" from a nearby shop. I called out to the seller and ordered three ice creams which cost ten rupees per piece. The seller slowly opened the lid of the container, grabbed three ice creams of orange, mango, and pineapple flavours, and handed them over to me. I gave it away to my father and Siyaram and kept the mango flavour one for myself.

I asked about his family members, his work, and so on while we were licking the ice cream just to get relief from the hot weather. I had not seen Jagan anywhere in the market, therefore, I thought of asking him about Jagan.

"How is Jagan *Khura*? I haven't seen him today. " I asked.

“He was suffering from cancer. Last month, he left this world.” He said.

“How are his family members now?”

“His wife is running a small tea stall in a market in our village. She stays alone at home.”

A beggar came to ask something when we were talking. I took out ten rupees from my purse and handed it over to him.

"Why have you given ten rupees? See, he is workable." Siyaram said to me.

"I don’t have coin," I replied.

Two customers were standing in front of us and asking the price per kilogram of brinjal. One of them bought one kg from my father.

The news of his death seemed to go through my veins. It deeply saddened me. Silently I prayed for his departed soul to journey to heaven and rest in peace.

As the weather was boiled by the sun, the thin white shirt that Siyaram wearing was getting wet. The stinky of his armpits travelling through the air was swirling in my nostrils. So, I maintained a little distance while I was talking with him. After talking for a few minutes, I came back home.

Dipen *Khura* bought leafy vegetables from others and resold them in the market. I was shocked when the man forcefully took the bundles of ferns from him. Because Dipen Khura will hardly earn two hundred rupees from all his leafy vegetables.

CHAPTER SIX

An Invisible Grass

Pangri flattened a small hilltop and made his house on it. At the bottom of the hill, there was a *kutcha* well from where they fetched the water. He made steps from the bottom to the top like a ladder to move up to their house. The air could freely enter his house, as it sat above the hill. The pine trees surrounding their yard were like sentinels, providing security from all sides. When the winter came and spread over a few months, the cold of that area always accelerated. Pangri had a daughter, Meenakshi and a pregnant wife Ka-et. He named his daughter after a movie actress. He didn't know what Meenakshi meant. Ka-et always fetched the water from that *kutcha* well and climbed the steps even though she was pregnant. Her three-year-old daughter always followed her wherever she went.

Pangri was not allowed to stay at his parents' home as he hadn't married his cousin (maternal cousin). He had disobeyed his parents by marrying Ka-et. Therefore, they were obliged to stay a little farther away from his parents. They didn't have any path to connect with the village. They had to walk through the bushes of grass and plants for about three kilometres to reach the village. So, in summer, when the weather was surrounded by stormy rains and the earth became wet everywhere, they faced the problem of even buying some essentials. However, in winter, they felt relief as the earth became dry. They could walk easily to different places.

Some members of an insurgency group were often seen in that area. Pangri's cousin, Atur, was also a member of that group. However, he hadn't returned to his home for 6 years. He joined the group when he was about 15 years old. His parents always expected his return as he was the only son. One early morning, around 4 a.m., there was a loud knock on the door. A voice called out "*Oh ni* (sister), *oh ni* (sister)," It was a freezing morning, and the fog made everything unclear. Ka-et was startled to hear someone's voice so early in the morning. Pangri got up, turned on the flashlight and opened the door. He saw a man wearing a light full shirt and carrying an A.K.-47 on his shoulder. He was shivering from the cold. Pangri recognised him as he often saw him in those areas.

"Come inside," Pangri said.

"Could you please light up the fire," He requested.

Pangri felt surprised by his behaviour. He thought he would order him. And as his wife was pregnant, he was afraid of him at first. But his calm behaviour made him easy to communicate with.

Pangri lit up the fire in the fire pit and let him sit beside it. Little Minakshi also stirred from his sleep.

Ka-et came from her room and said to Pangri, " Make tea,"

"Is there rice left in the kitchen?" The insurgent asked.

"There might be some leftover rice in the kitchen from last night," Ka-et replied.

"It's ok. Bring it here." He spoke.

She entered the kitchen, brought the leftover rice and handed them over. "There's no curry. You can roast dry fish" She said apologetically.

"It's ok." He replied.

She took out some dry fish from inside the bamboo tube and handed them over to him.

"It's too cold." He muttered.

"It's bitterly cold outside." Pangri sitting on the wooden stool beside him agreed.

The pungent aroma of roasted dry fish filled the room, wafting through the air and enveloping the surroundings. Anyone venturing out early in the morning would have been met with an unexpected and shocking culinary experience. Emboldened by his unexpectedly amiable demeanour, Pangri cautiously inquired about his cousin.

"I heard, my cousin, Atur, also joined your group 6 years ago. Do you know where is he now?"

He paused for a moment and said, "He is no more now. He was my friend."

Atur joined the group when his girlfriend left him and married another. During the training of the new members, he couldn't perform as other members did. At last, he tried to get away from the group. In the first attempt, he was caught and warned by the leader. In the second attempt, when the leader heard the news, he ordered his close friend to shoot him.

"Atur was shot by our leader." He said. Atur was shot dead by him indeed.

Slowly, his shivering got away as the flames of the fire warmed his body. His empty stomach also got to digest something as he finished the leftover rice. The pungent aroma of roasted dry fish was also cast away somewhere by the morning air.

Thousands of thoughts were running in Pangri's mind after getting his cousin's news. He got emotional but hid his expression in front of him.

"My uncle is still expecting his return," Pangri said.

"Nowadays, Armies are often visiting our places." He tried to avoid the topic.

Pangri understood his intention and why he came in the early morning.

When the darkness was swept away by the lights and the density of fogs diminished, he went to hide behind the standing hills.

Pangri waited inside his house for sunlight as he had to go to buy rice from a shop that was around four kilometres away from his home. He looked outside in between, but the sun was not seen yet. The area had only one grocery shop. Therefore, the seller always reduces consumers' surplus.

When the sun rose and its lights entered the house through small holes in a wooden window, he held a plastic bag and went out for the shop. He went through the bushes of grass which got wetted in night's dew drops and let his wife and daughter wait at home.

Ka-et held a steel pitcher and went down the steep steps to fetch water from the kutcha well. The well was dug beside a rock, like a small pond. A small spring fed the well and the overflow water was allowed to flow freely. As nobody lived in the nearby areas, the gurgling sound of the spring water filled the silent surroundings. Meenakshi cried, she thought she was left alone at home. She came to look for her mom towards the well.

"*Oh pei* (mom), *oh pei* (mom)," She screamed, cried and coughed.

"I am coming," Ka-et replied, holding a water full pitcher in her hand near the well.

Ka-et stepped up to the house with the water full pitcher and consoled her crying daughter. After keeping the pitcher in the kitchen, she went to look for the hungry oinking pigs in the pigpen. The pigpen was just beside their house, so the noxious smell always swirled through the air in the house. She thought she would arrange some food for the pigs when Pangri would arrive home. She went to pluck mastered greens from their small kitchen garden, washed them and kept them ready to cook.

Pangri crossed the Langso stream. When his bare feet touched the freezing water, it bit his legs. The chill coursed through his veins. He went through the village near his parents' home. When he crossed the house and saw his father looking at him for a while, but didn't say anything, he got emotional. His heart tried to say something but controlled himself. When he reached the shop and asked for 3 kg of rice, the seller, Ramesh, said in broken Assamese language in Hindi tune, "Kali apunar dewta bhi ahise. Apunalukor jamintu bikibo koise. (Your father also came here yesterday. He said he would sell your land)."

Pangri often went to buy from that shop since his childhood. So, he was well known to Ramesh.

"Oh, *hoi neki* (oh, is it)," Pangri responded. He didn't like to talk more about this topic.

When Pangri was ready to back home, his cousin, Angtong, also came to buy some grocery items in the shop. He was 2 years younger than Pangri.

"Yesterday, I met our uncle. He invited us to his home next Sunday. He asked me to tell you. Probably, they have a ritual that day." Angtong stated. His home was just beside Pangri's parents' house.

"I will try to go," Pangri replied, holding 3 k.g. of rice in his hand.

They talked for a few minutes and both left the place.

The sun's heat reduced the cold surroundings. Ka-et and Minakshi took sunshine in the yard. The hen and chicks also looked for their food around their house. The hen found a cricket, hence she clucked to call her baby chicks. The baby chicks ran towards their mother to grab it.

Pangri arrived home. Ka-et and Meenakshi also came inside the house.

"Uncle has invited us to their ritual." He informed his wife.

Meenakshi went to her father, held his fingers and tried to lean toward him.

"Which uncle?" Ke-at asked.

"Uncle Langtuk." He replied.

"When?"

"Next Sunday."

Pangri took a kettle, poured hot red tea into a bowl and sipped.

Ka-et, on the other side, took out some rice from the bag and poured it into a cooking pot, washed it and cooked it in the fire pit of the kitchen.

She boiled mustard greens and roasted dry fish. Meenakshi was fussy as she was hungry. A few doves sitting and cooing on the branches of trees seemed to calm her down. Ke-at also lit up the fire in the sideyard and boiled taro leaves for the hungry oinking pigs.

The next day, a dead body was found on the roadside. He was shot dead and thrown away on the road. Police came and took the dead body for postmortem. Everyone suspected the insurgent group. Pangri also got the news.

"Bitung was shot dead in the road," Pangri said to his wife.

Ka-et was shocked when she heard the news.

"Who shot him?" She asked.

"Probably, they (insurgents) did it. Sometimes, the insurgents do such acts individually. They demand money individually without the knowledge of the leader." He replied.

"A third person can do such an act sometimes. But, whoever did, it is a sad news for us." She said.

The house of Bitung was often visited by the police as he was the only man who could talk with them. He can speak Hindi and Assamese fluently. He studied up to 9th standard. Some people often suspected him as an informer for the police. People always sought his help when it came to official works. But, in return, he took charges from them.

Pangri had been coughing for a few days. He ate herbs to cure his cough, but it didn't work. The cold weather of those days kept constant his cough. He didn't have any jacket or sweater to wear in the cold morning. At night, when the weather got extremely cold, they often woke up and lit a fire in the fire pit to warm their bodies.

The Sunday arrived. Pangri got ready for his uncle's house in the morning. As his uncle's house was far away from his home and he had to come back home soon, so, he ate the last night's leftover rice. He wore a T-shirt that seemed to look new. He wore a *Choi Hongthor* above the t-shirt and wrapped a red *Poho* around his neck. Meenakshi hadn't woken up yet. She couldn't sleep well at night as his father was coughing almost all night. But, when her father stepped down from their home, she woke up, came out from inside and saw her father was going. She cried, wanted to go with him.

"*Chiru dari, chiru dari. Popo kut kut van po* (don't cry, don't cry. Your father will bring biscuit for you)." Her mother consoled her.

"*Kut kut vanpo dei muso* (honey, I will bring biscuits for you," Pangri asked her to stop crying.

Pangri went out to her uncle's house on foot. He felt a little guilty himself for being unable to take something with him for them. He walked on a narrow, curvy *kutch*a Road in the hills. *kutcha* road was the main road for hundreds of villages. The trees covering the hills seemed to look fresh as the dew drops wetted their leaves in the morning. He felt the trees standing beside the road belonged to him. He met some people on the road, too. Some were known, and some were unknown. When he was about to reach the destination, he saw that some people were also going that way. He could presume where those people were going. When he reached there, he saw his aunt welcoming the guests. When she saw him, she said, "Come inside."

"It's ok, Aunty. Where is the uncle? " He asked.

"He went to get a cock. He is probably coming now. Please be seated." She replied, welcoming other guests.

When Pangri was at home, he decided to share his cousin's news. But when he saw the celebration of the ritual, he changed his decision.

A few seconds later, his uncle arrived.

"Come to this side and hold it." He pointed the way and asked him to hold a red-coloured cock. The cock was bought and taken from their relative's house, which would be sacrificed in the ritual.

The time was noon. Some people were cooking rice and pork curry on the back side of their house. They made fire pits by digging the earth in the open spaces of their backyard. Pangri went to look there. The smoke of the fire along with the mouth-watering smell of the boiling curry was swirling and wafting through the air and spread to the side where guests were sitting. The chicken gravy was already cooked. Some men and women sat on the bamboo mat in a row. However, they sat separately. Some of the women sat with their children. Some of the children cried and some played. Some of the children ran here and there in the surroundings. The aged men and women sat on the other side. They were given special attention and respect.

A woman of about 40 years old, wearing a green colour *pekok* with black colour *amang* (decorative boundary of the *pekok*) and purple colour *pini*, uncombed curly hair and a little dark colour skin told the children, "Don't make noise, sit calmly children."

She was a neighbour who often led other women in different works of the village. She walked here and there and assisted the owner in arranging the programme.

Pangri found himself a little awkward sometimes as he was coughing frequently.

The time struck 1 O'clock. The main ritual was completed. Two young girls, both of them wearing *pekok, pini* and *vamkok*, came to distribute banana leaves to the guests sitting in a row. Two young boys distributed bamboo tubes. The owner offered full bottles of rice beer to some people as a sign of respect, some eagerly waited for the drops of beer in their glass. The hungry children rolled their eyes and waited for rice and pieces of meat in their dishes. The children beside their mother became restless, hinting at their hunger. A few moments later, two boys approached, carrying a large *karahi* and a bamboo ladle in their hand. They started to serve chicken gravy to everyone sitting there. One young man served the rice beer to the adult men and a few women. Another young man served water along with him. He served water to everyone sitting on the row. As the serving concluded, people began chanting their prayer, offering reverence to deities and invoking blessings for the hosts. One boy, about 7 years old, held a piece of chicken and started eating when his mother was chanting. Pangri also sat on the row and feigned chanting even though he didn't know the way of chanting. He looked at other people around silently. He anticipated that once someone began eating, he would follow suit. Upon the priest's cessation of chanting, the guests commenced to eat. They were also served rice and pork curry by those young boys and girls. The adult men drank the rice beer. Some of them sang songs lively, and some engaged in discussions about the traditions of different places when they became inebriated. A few women who became inebriated also took part with them. Pangri also had two full glasses of beer. He spoke more words and took part in the discussion after having the beer. The rays of the sun seemed to diminish, so, he looked at the sun. He decided to come back home. He met his uncle, aunt and other relatives at last and stepped back home.

Ka-et frequently looked toward the steps and waited for Pangri's arrival. Meenakshi played alone on the veranda and hummed the songs incorrectly in her tune.

"Is my father coming?" She asked.

"He is coming," Ka-et replied, even though she wasn't sure if he was coming or not.

"When will he arrive home?" She asked again.

"He will arrive soon." She replied.

The sun's rays seemed to come horizontally as it was about to descend on the horizon. The shadows of pine trees hid their house from the sun's rays. The goats freely grazing in the meadow also came home and roamed around the surroundings. When the sun set and the darkness began to fall, Ka-et heard the coughing sound of Pangri.

"Your father has arrived." She said to Meenakshi.

"*Oh po* (father)," Meenakshi exclaimed happily.

"*Muso*," Pangri responded.

Pangri came and sat beside Ka-et.

"Have you had your meal?" He asked.

She got the smell of rice beer when he opened his mouth.

"Why have you drunk the beer? Don't you know you have been coughing for a few days?" She rebuked him rather than answering his question.

"I drank just a little.".

"I know how much you drank."

"I thought it would reduce my cough." He tried to befool her.

"How will it reduce your cough." She replied angrily.

As the cold fell along with darkness in the evening, Pangri shivered a little. He went inside the kitchen, sat beside the fire pit and blew the air to raise the fire flame.

"I feel relaxed now." He expressed.

Meenakshi also sat beside him on a wooden stool and leaned toward her father.

"*Muso*, what have you eaten today?" Pangri enquired.

"*An Pen Han* (rice and curry)." She replied.

Ka-et came with a pot and said that she would cook rice. Pangri and Meenakshi sat just beside the fire, so she told them to sit a little distance.

"Why is your cough not cured yet? I am worried." She showed her worries.

"I don't know I cough more at night." He replied.

Ka-et lit up a homemade kerosene lamp. The lamp was made with a small bottle. The flies and insects came to the lighting lamp, so a lizard tried to come near the lamp to hunt the insects. When the rice and curry were cooked, they sat near the fire and had dinner.

The next day, at noon, Pangri felt a slight fever and decided not to go to the farmland. They cultivated ginger, broom, and chilli on the sloping hillside. He made a *Bitu Adap Dap* (a ladle-shaped tool to kill flies) from a young bamboo stick and began swatting flies in the house. When the flies landed on the floor, he used the *adap dap* to kill them. He tried to feed dead flies to the ants. When the ants swarmed to carry away the dead flies, he asked her daughter, Meenakshi, to come and look. As he stood up and cleared his throat, coughed up a small amount of blood. Frightened, he examined the blood carefully and told his wife that he had coughed up a trace of blood. His wife rushed over there, worried, and suggested that they should visit the priest. Pangri tried to suppress his cough, but he couldn't stop. He coughed again and saw more blood in it. He stayed thoughtfully for a second. His facial expression showed his startled and frightening situation. Ka-et turned pale for a while when she saw the blood again. The tears collected in her eyes and tried to fall down her cheeks. But when he coughed up again, the amount of blood in it reduced. Meenakshi was kept silent, probably she also could perceive the situation. Pangri asked his wife to bring hot water over there and sent Meenakshi to play the other side. He gurgled with warm water and a few moments later he said he would go to the priest.

The priest's house had a thatched roof, the kitchen was a stilt house and the boundary was made from bamboo sticks. Pangri entered the gate and enquired where the priest was. Two villagers were sitting and chatting there on the veranda. "We are also waiting for the priest." One of them replied.

"Have you come for any important work?" One of them who looked thin and tall asked.

Pangri narrated his condition.

"Once, my neighbour also suffered such a condition. I heard he was given *Bap* (The literal meaning of *Bap* is grass) by his relatives. He is cured now." Another one said. He was a little fat, but his height was short.

"The priest had given medicine to him." The thin one added.

The priest came out from the kitchen and asked all of them why they came.

Pangri narrated his condition to the priest.

"Someone might give you Bap." The fat one interfered.

"Did you go and eat something somewhere?" The priest asked.

"Yes, in my uncle, Langtuk's house yesterday," Pangri replied.

"I heard they have *Bap* in their home." The thin one said.

The priest brought everything needed for foresee, sat on the bamboo mat, arranged everything, chanted mantras and said, "Your relative gives you Bap."

Pangri didn't believe him, yet he pretended to believe him. He just asked for traditional medicine from the priest to treat the disease.

CHAPTER SEVEN

A Shadow Behind a Friend

"A good friend always helps a friend when a friend needs help" This quotation appeared on the first page when Mrinal was flipping a book given by his friend Prabin on a friendship day. When he saw the line, the slowest hand of the clock was pointing towards two, the mid-speed hand was towards twelve and the fastest hand was crossing twelve to reach this position again. It was Sunday afternoon in the winter season. The weather was also gloomy and cool. Mrinal took a soft spongy pillow under his head, lay down on his bed and covered a blanket below his neck. He combed the book that was decorated on the bookshelf. After combing a few pages, he fell asleep grunting a little sound from his nose.

The clock was ticking towards three when Prabin came to Mrinal's house. He looked around the house from outside and found all the doors closed except for a room. He approached closer, knocked at the opening wooden door and entered the room where Mrinal was sleeping. As the house was near a rice field, a little distance from the main inhabitant place, the surroundings were calm and quiet. The light wind entering through the opening uncurtained wooden window from the field was cooling the room. Mrinal didn't close the door and the window as his eyelids closed involuntarily after reading a few pages of the book. He had a very bad dream like someone was tightly pushing his neck down. He breathed heavily and then woke up. When he opened his eyes, he saw his friend Prabin sitting on a chair browsing his smartphone.

"When did you come?" Mrinal asked, wiping his eyes with his bare right palm.

"Just now," Prabin replied, putting his smartphone inside his pocket.

"How did you know our home?" He asked. "I heard someone was knocking on the door, but I could not open my eyes. I struggled a lot to shake my legs, but I failed. I don't know why it happens sometimes."

"Yes, sometimes it happens even to me. I went to your old home and asked your grandfather."

The house where Mrinal and his parents staying was newly constructed. It had a white tin roof and the walls were made of bamboo sticks, plastered with cow dung and earth on the bamboo sticks. The floor was plastered with soil and cement. The doors and windows were still not decorated with curtains. So, when Prabin went closer to the door, he could see directly inside the room. They stayed joint family with his uncle, Raju and grandparents before moving to that house. They didn't like to make their house adjacent to their uncle's house. They didn't have a convenient place to build their house near the village, therefore, they made their house a little distance from the village. However, even though the house was isolated from other villages, it was near a plastered road. Now his grandparents were staying with his uncle who got married a year before. Mrinal was shocked at first when he saw his friend Prabin sitting inside his room because he had not informed him before visiting there.

"You could have called me," Mrinal said.

"I have come for a different purpose. As I reached here, later I thought of visiting your home."

"Let me make tea, you sit for a while." Mrinal entered the kitchen and took a pan which dangled in a side of a rack. He turned on the filter's water tap, took water, turned on the gas stove and placed the pan on it.

His room was near the kitchen. Someone speaking in this room could be heard from the kitchen. “Where is your mother and father?” Prabin called out from the room.

"They have gone for a picnic with their friends. I am alone at home." Mrinal replied.

A few moments later, he brought two cups of tea on a tray with four pieces of Marie Biscuits and asked him to have it.

"I could have made an omelette if you are not vegetarian," Mrinal said. "This is your first visit after completing our college, right?”

“Yes, I could not manage my time after joining in bank. I have to work from morning 9 a.m. to evening 8.30. Today is Sunday and hence I come out to ride my Apache bike just to get relief from six days of headache.” Prabin replied.

As the paddy had already been cut and taken from the paddy fields a month before, hence, only the left-out dry straws were there in the fields. The light breeze blew and crossed the straws, entered through the window and flew out through the door outside.

"What are you doing nowadays?" Prabin enquired, sipping hot steaming tea from the cup after munching a biscuit.

"Nothing special, I teach some underprivileged children twice a week in the evening at least for one and a half hours, discussing with their parents, just trying to motivate both their parents and the children so that they are motivated towards education. Now, I am planning for agripreneurship. The land lying backside of our house around 21 bighas is our land. They have not been properly used till now. We cultivate paddy in one season and in the rest, it lies vacant."

"You teach the children of this village?"

"No, very remote area, it is ten kilometres away from this village. You know Prabin, my parents often rebuke me for not applying for government jobs. I don't know why I seek freedom in my life. Therefore, I want to be an entrepreneur." Mrinal expressed his view. He took a packet of cigarettes from a bag hiding behind his clothes hanging at the cloth stand. His clothes looked very messy on the cloth stand. He took out a cigarette, lit up and smoked after finishing his tea.

"Don't your parents scold you for the smoking?"

"I don't let my parents know."

Prabin didn't sit much time after finishing his tea. He looked outside from the window, looked up at the unclear sky and decided to go back to his home.

Longki, Prabin and Mrinal have been friends since their college days. All of them stayed at a rented house on the same campus. It was a silver colour painted three-storey building with wooden colours tiles in the rooms where the owner stayed on the ground floor with his wife and his sole daughter Meera. Both Longki and Mrinal studied honours in sociology with an economics pass course. Mrinal was sociable and extrovert nature; therefore, he could make friends easily with the people. On the other hand, Prabin was a little introvert who studied mathematics honours with an economics pass course. He was often praised by the teachers for his studiousness, discipline and excellence in academics. He was a vegetarian and often stayed away from parties. Longki and Mrinal, on the other hand, often had parties with their friends, they drank beer with chicken, pork and sometimes with a mixture of *Chana*. Prabin enjoyed only the *Chanas* when he came to join the party once in a blue moon. When they got drunk, their voices increased, and they sang and danced sometimes up to 1 or 2 A.M. Sometimes, the landlord did scold them when they made excessive noise. During the party, when Mrinal's girlfriend Urmila wanted to talk with him on the phone, he pretended to be normal. He tried to speak in a lower tune to straighten his curvy voice. When he felt dizzy because of alcohol's stinging, he pretended to be very sleepy and tried to hang up his phone. Sometimes he slept without hanging up his phone while talking with Urmila. They took their dinners after finishing the alcohol. When the participants were more than the dishes available, some of them ate even on the lid of cooking pots and also on the pots themselves. When Urmila tried to spend with him on the phone during the ongoing party, he asked everyone to keep silent for a while pretending to be very busy with writing assignments. He, sometimes, was obliged to eat on the pressure cooker when the utensils fell short and parties were arranged in his room. Arun who studied in a different college also stayed on the upper floor of the same building. He didn't like to contribute to the parties even though he drank more alcohol than all of them.

It has been five years now since the completion of his college. Mrinal kicked started his dream project at their land. One day, he felt tired, so he kept the pillows aside, lay down on an L-shaped sofa, and kept his head on the inside arm. The television was already turned on by his mother. She played old Bollywood songs and made a cool and nostalgic environment for her. He picked up the remote control that was lying on the centre table and then changed the channels in it. He felt tired because he worked on their land with the labourers. He planted different kinds of local fruits in three bighas of land, coconut in two bighas, areca nuts in two bighas, and some valuable woods in three bighas till then. The rest two bighas had been kept empty for seasonal vegetables, four bighas of land for fishery, and two bighas for restaurants where people can read different kinds of books along with every sip of hot tea or coffee. Because he wanted to make a unique kind of library which would be mixed up with the restaurant and park. The people who would visit the campus can study everywhere. Two bighas for a playground and one bigha for his own house where his family members and other security personnel would be staying. His father had taken a personal loan from a bank to assist his son's dream project. Earlier his father didn't like to support him, he expected his son to be a government employee as every parent expects. But later, he started encouraging him, asking about problems and discussing with him.

He saw a familiar face on the television screen while he was changing the channels. He got up hastily, and with an intent to see again, he pressed the button for the reverse direction. He saw the very shocking and horrible news on a regional news channel. The news anchor was shouting and yelling, flashing the face of his friend on the TV screen very frequently. He couldn't believe the news at first.

"Mom, come here, come fast." He called out his mother.

"What happened?" She replied from the kitchen. His mother was frying *pokora* to have with evening sugarless red tea. His parents did not like milk tea, they liked to have a little bitter red tea. Therefore, they hardly made milk tea at their home.

"Come fast." Persisted again.

His mother brought two cups of steaming red tea on a tray and hot *pokora* in a red rose-imprinted white clay bowl. She kept the bowl on the wooden dining table.

"Look at the news Mom." Mrinal pointing towards the television screen.

"What happens to him?" She uninterestingly asked.

"Look at the television screen properly."

His mother was dumbstruck by looking at the news because she met him thrice when his son was studying in college. Shockingly, she kept looking at the screen. She felt terrified as his son often talked to him through the phone. Mrinal asked everything about the procedures to him when his father wanted to take a personal loan from a bank.

The news baffled him; therefore, he dialled up to his friend Karan. Karan was his classmate who often mingled with the girls. Except in the girls' washroom and the common room, he often stayed with girls in the college. Some girls even shared their problems with Karan. But the interesting was that he couldn't make a girlfriend for himself.

"Hello *dost*, do you still remember me?" Karan said on the phone.

"Dost, I miss you all sometimes. How are you?" He didn't ask about the news at first.

"I am fine. I have seen your ex-girlfriend Urmila with a man probably he was her husband." He jested.

"Dost please, I don't like to remember her. I dialled up for a different purpose. I have just watched the news; I do not believe in news channels nowadays. Therefore, I have called you to know the news of Pookia. Is the news true?"

"What news? I don't have any contact with him nowadays." Karan asked back with an eagerness to know about the news.

"I thought you would have the information. Let me ask Gela."

Mrinal didn't explain to him what he had seen in the news. As the hot crunchy veg *pokora* and the deep red tea were ready, he sat at the dining table, grasped a few *pokora* from the bowl, and crunched them with every sip of the tea. He didn't believe any news channels easily, but later he thought this kind of news might be true. When he browsed his Facebook and scrolled the news feed, he found it on different news pages. He was inquisitive to dig out the news, therefore, he stood up, left the rest of the *pokora* and tea on the table and dialled up to his friend Gela.

"Finish the *pokora*." His mother who was sitting on the one side of the four-seater dining table urged him. He didn't lend his mind as his mind was investigating the news of Pookia.

"Hello, what's up buddy?" Gela said

"Where are you?"

"I am here at home."

"Do you know about the news of Pookia? I have just seen it on a news channel. Is the news true?"

" It is true. I have gone to see him when the police were arresting him."

"I am shocked to see him on the news channel."

"Really. Even though we were not allowed to go closer to him, still I could recognize the pieces of human legs and arms which were unearthed by the police from his kitchen."

"Shocking incident! He pretended to be a vegetarian. All right, I called you to ascertain the news." Mrinal disconnected his phone.

"I have never heard the names Pookia, and Gela from your mouth. Who are they?" His mother asked him as she already finished tea and *Pokora* of her part.

"These are the nicknames given by our friends. The nickname of Prabin is Pookia and Arun is Gela. Prabin is a bookworm, so we call him Pookia and Arun often bunked the classes and drank alcohol drinks at night, so we named him Gela." He replied, sighed and sat again at the dining table.

Six Years Later. A part of Mrinal's land is filled with young and charming plants whose branches are wearing with green leaves. The thin areca nut plants standing straight up are bearing fruits whose leaves are trying to look to their roots. The coconut plants with huge trunks sitting on the ground are preparing themselves to bear their fruits. As per his planning, different fishes are playing and jumping in the water of the ponds. The different species of birds come and take rest on the trees as fruits dangling from the branches and twigs always invite them. Their chirpings make the music of nature in the whole surroundings. The restaurants cum library attracts people from different places. The whole area becomes a park as he keeps the area very clean.

CHAPTER EIGHT

A Girl Behind a Curtain

A girls' hostel often filled with *Addas* fell into a quiet environment. The hostellers' eyes started to screen the pages of long abandoned books. Some students flipped the pages without making any sounds in their mouths, while some others made hissing-like sounds, and tried to transmit the writings to their memories. It was an examination period. The examinations of some students were almost finished, while some others' examinations had just started. Sintu was packing her belongings to move back to her home. A few things, like toothpaste, toothbrush, soap, face cream and her college dresses were left unpacked because the next day was her last examination of B.A. final semester. She had to wear the college's dresses for the next day's examination. She took honours in English Literature and would appear for American Literature in her last day examination. She picked up a compass from Kabon's table and scratched it on the wall to make her name just beside her bed. Her roommate, Kabon was also appearing in her 2nd-semester examinations, but hers would be finished one week later. She was studying BSc with honours in chemistry. She had already finished her paper on organic chemistry. Her upcoming examination will be on inorganic chemistry.

It was a Sunday in June. The weather was very hot. The scorching sun heat was boiling them up in the concrete room. The air flowing out of the ceiling fan was like came after rolling through the fire flames. Staying on the top floor of a three-storey building was like a punishment for them. Kabon opened the small sliding window to let the outside scarce winds enter the room. The window grills looked like a prison fence. Sintu was drenched in sweat. Her light white T-shirt was pasted on her body skin. Even though Kabon also assisted in packing her belongings, she didn't sweat as Sintu did. Most of the girls on the top floor came down to the ground floor to get relief from the burning heat. A few of them took a rest under the shade of a banyan tree standing beside the hostel building.

The next day, in the morning, it was raining. The sound of the chirpings of birds and the pattering sound of raindrops spread the entire room. The mewling of winds entering through the corridor knocked on the door and tried to enter the room. Sintu got up, cast her eyes on the door and started to study for the exam. When the clock was ticking the 8.30 a.m. She got ready and stepped out for the examination. At 8.50 a.m., she got both a writing sheet and question paper from the allotted invigilators. When the hour hand pointed towards nine and the minute hand towards twelve, she folded the writing sheet from three sides and started to write her examination. She kept large spaces between the lines even after folding from three sides probably she thought it was the trick to get better marks.

Her exam was over at noon and so, came back to her hostel. It was still raining, but its density decreased. Her father took a rest in a room in front of the hostel along with some guardians of some hostelers. They also came to pick their daughters up from the hostel. He was drenched. The black spots which often hid in his dry white shirt were seen now. The stinking smell also released from his armpits.

"When did you reach here, father?" Sintu asked her father, holding and pulling her trolley.

"Around half an hour ago." He replied, wiping his face with a damp handkerchief.

"Are you feeling hungry?"

"I had tea and *Samosa* in a hotel." Her father replied.

Sintu dialled a cab driver's number and told him to drop them up at the bus stand.

Three months later, she graduated and she wanted to stay away from her home.

"Father, I want to prepare for competitive examinations. I want to take coaching in Guwahati." Sintu requested her father.

Her father was sitting on a chair reclining toward the back. Her mother was sitting on a wooden stool beside him. She was kneading flour to bake cookies. Her brother, Munjin, was busy watching reels on Facebook in his room.

"I don't have any problem if you prepare seriously." Her father replied.

"Whom with will you stay in Guwahati?" Her mom asked, holding steel *Gamla* with her left hand tightly and kneading the flour with her right hand.

"With my classmate. Her name is Reena," Sintu replied.

Two weeks later, after getting the nod from her parents, Sintu moved from Biswanath to Guwahati city. In the morning 7 O'clock, her father dropped her up at the ASTC bus stand. She booked a ticket from the ticket counter; and waited for the bus. The red and white colour super bus arrived at the exact given time. The conductor got down and shouted "Gohati, Gohati, Gohati" loudly. Sintu asked the conductor to keep her luggage inside the luggage compartment and got on the bus. Other passengers also got on the bus and sat in their allotted seats. A few seconds later, the engine of the bus started roaring. The driver chewing a mouthful of betel nut spat from the window and rolled the steering wheel to move ahead. Sintu opened the window as she sat on a window seat. The bus was moving at an average speed. She pushed the recline lever and adjusted her seat. The bus was moving and when it was about to reach Bharali Bridge, one of her fellow passengers who sat just beside her seat was mincing tobacco in his palm. She snitched as the scent released from tobacco entered her nostrils. The bus had stopped at Mission Chariali for ten minutes and again started to move for Guwahati. When they reached Amoni, the bus stopped near a hotel to let the passengers have their meal. A lady passenger almost her age sitting just in her front seat vomited. She splashed vomitus over the bus. The odour released from the vomitus circled inside and travelled through the air. Sintu took her white cotton scarf and covered her nose.

Two days later, around 9 p.m., both of her parents already had their dinner. They were sitting on the cushionless wooden sofa in the drawing room. Her mother was cutting betel nuts with *Kotari* after washing utensils. Her father, on the other hand, was leaning towards the back, resting his head on the top of the sofa. His big bulging stomach seemed to like pushing his backbone towards the back.

"Do you know Sintu's friend?" Her mother asked.

"How will I know her college friend."

"Do you know her?" He asked back.

"No, I don't know. I am worrying about Sintu." She replied.

"Don't worry our daughter is mature now. She won't do anything wrong." He assured her, taking one piece of betel nut, betel leaf and a little slaked lime.

Her mom was caught in a net of perplexing thoughts. She took her keypad mobile phone and dialled up her daughter.

"Hello." Said in a loud voice as if her daughter wouldn't be able to hear her voice.

"Yes, mom." Sintu held her phone a little distance from her ear. She knew her voice would be loud.

"Are you in your room?"

“Where would I go; I am in my room.”

“Have you eaten your dinner?”

"No Mom, I am studying." Sintu pretended to be studious. She was watching a movie on her laptop.

“Study well; we have just had our dinner.”

“Is everything good at home? “

“Yes, we are fine here.”

“Mom, I want to enrol for coaching, I need twenty thousand rupees.” Sintu made a way to grasp money from her parents. The cost of the coaching was indeed seven thousand rupees only.

"OK, I will tell your father. Now, I hang up the phone." Her mother winded up her talk with her daughter.

Four years later, Sintu was still staying in Guwahati city. She stayed with Manuj instead of Reena. Reena then worked as a probationary officer in a public sector bank. Sintu, on the other hand, still did not know how to apply for a post online. When her parents called her on the phone and asked about her preparation for the exam, she always made a story to escape from the questions.

One day, it was Sunday at 7 p.m. Her father just arrived home. He went to buy vegetables and other grocery items from the daily market. Most of the shops in the town were closed except a few shops in the daily market. The places with a high density of heads, bicycles, and motorcycles turned spacious that day. The prices were skyrocketing and hence, buying sufficient items for the kitchen was difficult. Her mother had a meeting for their self-help group and had to pay three hundred rupees for her monthly contribution. So, she took the money and went to the meeting. That night, it was 10 p.m., and they were having dinner; all of them sitting on the floor. Her mother placed carpet on the floor and all of them sat on it. Her father was talking about the burning prices of commodities while everyone was chewing the white rice and yellow dal in their mouths. Their dishes also had potato and French bean bhaji.

"We should be very economical this month. After deducting the home loan and personal loan, the left out has been used for Munjin's admission and Sintu's house rent." Her father expressed thoughtfully.

"Why is sister Sintu staying in Guwahati without doing anything," Munjin said, swallowing a mouthful of rice.

"Exactly, we have to call her at home. At least our unnecessary expenditure would be lessened." His mother showed her support.

"I don't think that she is seriously preparing for competitive examinations," Munjin said again. Even though he was six years younger than her sister, still he was more mature than Sintu in many aspects. He didn't want to study in a private college, his father enrolled him in a private college.

"You are right, we have to call her." His father said after thinking deeply for a while.

"She cannot operate even a basic computer; how would she apply for examinations?" Munjin added.

The discussion lasted almost twenty minutes. Now all of them agreed to call her back.

One month later, Sintu left Guwahati city. She left bars and restaurants at which she occasionally visited with Manuj. She brought the memories created in Nehru parks, Dighali Pukhuri, the zoo and many different places in the city. She stayed with her parents at home after back from Guwahati. Everyone at their home slept at around 10.30 p.m. and got up at around 6 a.m. After having dinner, when everyone closed their doors, Sintu closed her door too. But when everyone snoring in their sleep, she opened her window facing towards the yard and started to light up the cigarette. She inhaled the smoke of cigarettes and exhaled them outside the window. She always browsed her mobile phone till 2 p.m. and sometimes more than that and got up after 9 a.m. One day, when everyone went out of home, she lit up incense sticks and then smoked a cigarette. She lit up an incense stick to spread its fragrance to wipe up the smell of cigarettes.

"Why are you lighting up the incense stick at this time?" Munjin enquired. He found himself inhaling the smell of cigarettes along with the fragrance of the incense stick together. The mixed smell travelled through the air and spread throughout the entire room. He got confused about who had smoked the cigarette. That day was Sunday. He didn't have his class, so went to his classmate Binong's house and then back home. Their parents, however, went to the farmland.

"Mosquitos were humming in my room. So, I lit up to let them flee from the room." She replied gingerly, probably thinking she would be caught.

"Why its smell is like the smell of a cigarette?" He asked sceptically.

"I don't know why; it is of new arrival in the shop. I haven't checked the name of the company." She replied cunningly.

Munjin switched on the ceiling fan and opened the window of his room to let them go outside with the air. The backside door was also closed, so he went to open it too and then came out to the veranda. He sat on the lounge chair at which his father always sat while he took a rest.

Her mother always told her to get up soon in the morning, yet she didn't lend her ears. When she rebuked her in a loud voice, Sintu made louder and kept her mother silent. Now she just wanted to leave her in someone's hand who would take care of her.

One night, it was a full moon night. Everyone was sitting in the courtyard under the splendid moonlight. The weather was neither cool nor hot. They were enjoying the stars illuminating their lights in the clear sky. The time was even ticking nine, some birds resting on the nearby standing Indian Rose Chestnut tree were twittering with immense joy. A mother goat who often bleated at night was sleeping happily in the shadow of that tree. She could see her newborn babies under the sprinkling moonlight. Sintu was sitting and exchanging words with them. She frequently checked messages on her smartphone. They sat there for around half an hour and then all entered into the dining room to have dinner. That night, they all were sitting at the dining table. Her father brought local Ari fish from the daily market. Her mother boiled that fish with tomato. She put the pasted green chilli and a little ginger and garlic. As she put sliced onion with tomato, hence the curry became yummier. At around 9 PM, when everyone went to sleep, she closed the door and opened the window. She inhaled the smoke of cigarettes behind the curtain and exhaled them outside the window through her two nostrils.

CHAPTER NINE

Under a Rusted Tin Roof

Sarpong lived with his parents and sister in a small village, Rongkhang. They lived in an old and rusted tin-roofed small hut. The hut had a single door, and two windows and partitioned to make two separate rooms. The door and windows were made of split bamboo sticks. They always kept strong bamboo sticks beside the door and windows for locking and unlocking them. A rope was always tied in the middle of doors and windows. When they closed them, the bamboo sticks were put in the tying ropes to support the closing door or windows. The walls of the house were also made of split bamboo sticks and they were plastered with a mixture of clay and cow dung. They also had a container-shaped, low tin-roofed small kitchen beside their hut. But they hadn't plastered the mix of cow dung and clay on that wall. We could see the outside view from inside through the narrow spaces between the sticks. If we peep from the outside, we could see everything inside. When the sun sprinkled its rays in the morning, the beams of light entered the kitchen through the spaces between the bamboo sticks.

Sarpong was studying B. Com in a college which was 20 kilometres away from his home. He went to the college by bicycle. In the evening, he gave tuition to the school students of his village, Rongkhang. His sister, Kadom, was studying in class ten in a school near their village, Rongman. As she was good at studying, her school teachers often visited their home to counsel, encourage and motivate her as well as to her parents. Sarpong, on the other hand, was an average student who also took responsibility even of her sister's study expenses. They didn't have any wooden beds and tables. They made their bed with split bamboo and then dried thatches placed on them to make them a little spongy. Sarpong made his small bed in the kitchen as they had only two rooms. One room was for his parents and another one was for Kadom. They had a three-foot bench and two plastic chairs to sit on. One day in summer, the weather was mercilessly hot and the wind couldn't even shake the leaves of trees. The electricity was also not available, connection had been cut for one week. I heard many of the households hadn't paid their bills for the last six months. I went to their home in the evening around 8 O'clock when the sun already hid itself from the sky and the darkness started to devour its rays.

"Brother, please be seated." Sarpong pulled a chair towards me.

"You don't have tuition today?" I asked him, after sitting on the chair.

"No. I am not feeling well." He replied, sitting on the wooden bench beside me.

In our village, we visit our neighbours without any reason. Sometimes they do come and sometimes we go to their houses. If we have to call our neighbours, we often directly shout from our homes rather than to go their homes. They reply to us like we do.

We were sitting outside their home; it was in their yard. The crickets were chirping and the fireflies were flickering their lights in our surroundings. A charger light congregated by the flies was also flickering probably the charge would be over. I was sitting on the chair, inhaling the air under the open sky scattered with twinkling white stars. The pale moon encircled by the thin white cloud was looking like beaming amidst some dust particles. I was given a hand fan and hence, I was fanning my face to get relief from the scorching hot. I was wearing a vest and half pant. My armpits surrounded by axillary hair were also sweating. When we were having the conversation, one leg of the chair where I was sitting suddenly broke down. I fell and my head was hardly pressed to the ground, but luckily, I was fine.

"This has happened owing to my overweight," I said.

“How much is your weight?” Kangbura asked, sitting on a *Peera* (low-height wooden stool) and mincing tobacco on his palm.

They always sat on the *peera* when they ate their meal. In winter, when the cold embraced us especially, in the morning and evening, they sat on the stools and encircled the fire.

“130 KG.” I laughed.

“Bah!" he expressed in shock.

He was very thin; his weight was much lesser than what ought to be as per his height. I was, on the other hand, overweight. My belly fat was tilting to the ground. I was always afraid of my obesity, but still, I could not maintain a proper diet. I heard people in our village call me gourmand.

After talking with them for around half an hour I came back home. When I reached home, the smell of pork curry with bamboo shoots wafted through the air. I could imagine how it would be tasty and yummy. My health concern was lost somewhere after inhaling the delicious smell of bamboo shoots with pork.

They hadn't bought a new chair even after a month. When somebody went to their home, they let them sit on a bench. If the bench cannot accommodate them, then they let them sit on the wooden stools. The bench was stained with slaked lime because when people ate the slaked lime with betel nut, the rest sticking at their fingers were rubbed at the bench to keep their fingers clean. The bench looked very dirty.

Our village was always filled with filthy politics. When the news of the election entered the village, some obsequious people of the parties went to every household at night to pull towards their side. They made promises in the sweetest words nesting in their tongue. The face-off between the parties often made the worse environment everywhere. The fracas between the two brothers sometimes compelled them to knock on the door of the court. Some sycophants distributed wine as well as *Sulai* to get the vote of some drunkards. The drunkards sold their vote in exchange for a glass of wine. When they got red *Bilati wine*, probably they felt lucky enough, because they usually drank *Sulai*. On the day of the election, the local leaders of a party kept their pockets full of notes so that they could drop something into the mouths of some people. When the party meetings were organised, the supporters went to lend their ears to the lectures of their leaders. Some people were unable to understand their languages, but still, they went to keep their feet on the meeting ground. On the day of counting, they thronged near the counting office, made their ears stand like the ears of a rabbit, and celebrated by beating drums and utensils when their leaders got the votes ahead of their opponents.

One day, I went to cast my vote around 10 a.m. I stopped at a *Paan* shop and bought a piece of betel nut and a loosie of cigarette. I chewed betel nut, lit the cigarette and smoked. Near the paan shop, a hotel which usually sold tea and biscuits every day sold rice and roti that day. The hotel was rather booked by a political party. The local leaders asked the voters to visit the hotel and served the meals free to get their votes in their favour. I was also asked to have rice with chicken, but as I didn't want to be involved with any party, I sought an excuse.

When a party won, the obsequious people of the winning party grasped all the benefits. The government schemes often streamed down to the granaries of these obsequious people. Some poorest of the poor who should be entitled to the benefits often got deprived of them.

Uncle Kangbura came to our home a few days later. I let him sit on a chair in our front corridor. Electricity was already resupplied by the company two days before, therefore I switched on the fan and sat under a moving fan.

"I come to seek your help," He said before we asked him.

"What kind of help?" I asked.

"I need two thousand rupees for an important work. I will repay you three weeks later."

I didn't ask about his important work. I thought whether it would be in my purse or not. Two days before, I withdrew three thousand rupees from an ATM. I already spent some amount. Hence, I was not sure.

"Let me check my purse." I let him wait.

The fan moving above our heads was making noise. It was roaring, probably it needed an electrician. It was disturbing our conversation.

"You haven't got a dwelling house?"

“Not yet.”

“Why? Haven’t you sought from Kungri?”

“Kungri is just the namesake for the post. Her husband does every work of the Sarpanch. He just let her put her signature on the files. See, how they are making two storeys building in four years. This is her last year. “

“You could have requested to our ward member.”

“She cannot even put her signature properly. Still, I requested her thrice. Now, I don’t like to request her.” He sadly expressed.

“This is one of the major problems in our village. People are politically not aware. Our Gram Panchayat is always run by a few people. They are grabbing most of the public money and putting them inside their pockets. See, how these people are making their houses.” I agreed with him.

“Abhinav has recently got a government job. Do you think he got this job on merit? No. He got this job because his father has a good relationship with our local MLA. He told my son when he came to our home." He added.

My mom brought two glasses of cold drinks on a tray. She bought a litre bottle of cold drink from the market that day. She took out from the refrigerator and poured in glasses. She was listening to our conversation even though she was mopping the floor inside. After finishing her work, she came out with glasses of cold drink.

“Is my sister fine?” She asked about his wife.

“Yes, she is good." He replied. "She has gone to work at a tea estate. She might be coming now." He added.

"How does she go? Can she ride a bicycle?"

“No, she can’t. A mini truck picks them up in the morning around 7 O’clock and drops them in the evening. Probably, it was the company’s truck.” He said, holding the glass of cold drink in his right hand.

I drank and got relieved for a while as it was roasting hot even though we were under the moving fan.

"Please have cold drink." My mom said.

“Ok, thank you. I am letting it a little warm.”

“You can drink slowly.”

“Go and get tobacco from the table there.” My mom said to me.

We didn’t consume tobacco at home, but we kept it at home, especially for people like Kangbura uncle. When such people visited our home, we offered them betel nuts and tobacco. That day, we didn’t have betel nut, that’s why, my mom sent me to get tobacco. Offering betel nuts and tobacco to the people who visit our home was a common practice in our village. My grandmother ate tobacco, slaked lime and betel nut together; therefore, her teeth were turned into black colour. But, after her death, we hadn’t any members in our family who consumed those items.

“I have been discussing about politics of our village with Nitur.” He diverted the topics.

“It feels sad if we look at the situation," Mom replied.

My mom also took part in the discussion on politics. We were discussing corruption which was happening at the grassroots level. How the conflicts and fighting happened among the people of the same village. How the obsequious people could do anything under the order of their leaders. How those people moulded and deceived the innocent public.

One day, the day before the election, I saw some people distributing five KG of salt to every household in our area. We had a total of twenty households. That day, in the morning around 8 O'clock, I was riding a bicycle to buy a few things from a grocery shop. One of them called me out from a little distance. I didn’t know why he called me.

Hence, I went closer to them by paddling the bicycle.

"Take 5 packets from here." He pointed towards the packets. One packet contained one kg of salt.

I stood still and thought for a while. I could understand why they were distributing salt to every household.

"Thank you. We don't need salt. We have already bought yesterday." I replied politely and went back.

As my father was a government employee, we didn't get any direct benefits from the panchayat. My mom was interested in knitting, weaving and sewing activities. Once she applied for weaving tools at the gram panchayat, but the sarpanch rejected her application, saying that we had a government employee. That year the sarpanch was male. Since then, we haven't applied for any welfare schemes that are usually provided in villages.

I counted their total expenditure. If the price of per kg salt is ten rupees, it means they had given fifty rupees per household to get their votes. I had seen some of the people happily receiving them. But I didn't want to disclose our names to the public just for fifty rupees in the name of votes.

One year later, it was an evening in summer. The black thick clouds hid the sun behind them. The sun's rays could not pass through the thick layer of the clouds and hence our surroundings became darker as if the sky falling on our heads. After a while, the rains started to drumbeat on the ground. The goats grazing in the pasture ran towards their shed. They were bleating inside, probably, they couldn't fill their hollow stomach yet. The cattle, on the other hand, were showering themselves in the splashing rains. Our cow and her calf were tethered in the pasture. So, I grabbed an umbrella and went hurriedly to bring them back to their shed. When I saw they were mooing and staring at me. I untethered them and let them go to their shed.

The next morning, the weather seemed a little clearer. We could see the sun sprinkle its rays, green leaves deriving energy from the sun's rays looked fresh. A couple of Myna sitting on the roof of our house were twittering in joy. As the sun was sprinkling its rays, my mom took out two bags of rice grain from the granary and spread them out on a bamboo mat to get dry.

"It seems the rain will pour again," I said to my mom.

"If we do not let them dry, we won't have rice to eat after two days." She replied.

That day at around 1 p.m., the weather changed. Again, the black cloud started floating in the sky. The sun seemed to step back behind the clouds. My mom asked me for help to gather the spread of rice grains. Around twenty minutes later, it was pouring hailstorms. At first, the hails were small size. We thought it would be as usual, therefore, we didn't take it seriously. Children near our house were shouting, enjoying picking them up. But later, big size of hails started patting on our tin roofs. They made a huge noise while patting on. The tin roof of the kitchen was old and rusted, it couldn't resist the hails and hence, turned into a Japanese sieve. Around half an hour later, the hails stopped patting on and the density of raindrops diminished. I was sure some of the households would suffer more than us. I opened an umbrella to protect myself from the arrowing rain and went out to see other houses.

"How is the tin roof of your house?" I asked one of our neighbours.

"The tin roof of the kitchen is damaged." He spoke.

They had roofed a new green colour tin in their newly constructed house. Therefore, I knew their roof wouldn't be affected. However, the tin roof of their kitchen was as

rusted as ours.

“Sarpong, Sarpong...” I shouted from the road.

"Sarpong has gone to work in a truck," Kadom replied from the veranda. She was a little wet. Sarpong often went to work in trucks as a labourer. I opened the *Nongola* and went to see their house.

"Our roof is damaged." Kangbura came out from their kitchen and said.

“Our kitchen’s roof is also damaged," I said.

Even though our tin roof was also damaged in hailstorms, I was worrying more about their condition. The facial expression of Kangbura raised thousands of questions in my mind.

CHAPTER TEN

A Dunkard's Wife

It was Sunday in the mid-winter. The drizzling rain was quenching the thirst of the dry weather. Some yellowish tree leaves were falling off to the ground as the gentle breeze came blowing with the rain. The dusty roads were also enjoying the raindrops as they got to shower themselves after a couple of weeks. The trees were overjoyed and felt relief in that falling rain. Their leaves were waving and dancing with the whooshes of the wind. The sun which sprinkles its rays in winter was shielded by a thick layer of dark clouds. I was coming from Kangdak town to my home, listening to 80's Bollywood songs that were played in my white colour Alto car. The wiper on the glass kept sweeping the raindrops seemed to dance with the rhythms of music. The cool wind too entered through a window as I kept it open a little. Its swirling sound seemed to hiss in my two ears. I was driving alone and enjoying the music. When the rolling wheels splashed the rainwater and made a sound, it seemed to reduce the sound playing inside the car. I saw a woman selling fresh local vegetables, and forest herbs on the roadside. She was drenched, perhaps she didn't cover herself with an umbrella when she came from her home. She was selling those items under the shade of a temporarily made small tin-roofed vendor.

Precipitously, I stopped my car near the shop and got down to buy *Mehek* leaves *(a kind of forest herb)* as it was not available in our village. The pitter-patter sounds of the raindrops seemed to create a noise. The blowing wind conjoined with the falling raindrops was freezing that day. Standing in front of her shop under the shade of the roof I asked the price per bundle of the *Mehek* leaves.

"Ten rupees *Ik* (brother). It is fresh, just plucked from the forest." The woman replied gently.

She wore a daintily woven blue colour *Pekok*, black colour *Pini* and purple colour *Vamkok (Pini, Pekok* and *Vamkok* are the traditional dresses of Karbi women). The finely designed hems of the *Pekok* made more attractive to her dress. She hung a sky-blue colour *Jamborong* (bag) around her neck to keep her money inside.

A boy around 8 years old was sitting beside her. He was wearing a purple colour pant and a white colour shirt. Perhaps he was feeling cold and hence, shivering a little in that cool weather. The dresses seemed to be like his school dress. I could sense their financial condition by looking at them.

"Is he your son?" I asked the woman.

"Yes, he is. I have three children. Two girls and one boy. He is the youngest." She replied.

"Does he go to school *Ni* (sister)?" I eagerly asked her again.

"Yes, he does. He is studying in class four. Today is Sunday, nobody is at home, therefore I could not leave him alone. My elder daughter is studying at a college. She stays in a rented house and the second one is studying in class 10. She stays at her uncle's house." She replied without any hesitation.

Amidst exchanging our words, I saw a group of young girls coming towards the road from the hillside. They were carrying *Hak* (a kind of Karbi's traditional goods carrying basket. It is generally made of cane and bamboo) on their back. While they came closer to us, I asked them about what they were carrying inside their *Haks*.

"*Hanthu* and *Henru*." One of them replied timorously.

Hanthu is a kind of forest herb which is very popular in Karbi's cuisine. Arum leave is called *Henru* in the Karbi language. While they were crossing us, I was trying to capture them with the lens of my Samsung smartphone. The pictures flashing on my phone's screen took me back to my childhood days. I used to go with my friends sometimes for forest herbs, sometimes for fishing in the rivulets. When we felt hungry, we often ate different kinds of edible fruits found in the forest. When we felt thirsty, we drank directly from the flowing streams and rivulets. When the water became murky and clayey, especially in summer, we searched the sandy banks of the rivers and dug either with our bare hands or knives. We knelt, touched our mouths to the water and drank. I clicked a few photos as photography is one of my hobbies. I find happiness when I get to snap photos of some special moments. Sometimes, I do think that if wildlife photography is my profession, I may not be able to earn as I do now, but, surely, I will get immense happiness.

I took out thirty rupees from my purse and gave her for the exchange of three bundles of *Mehek* leaves. She took the money, checked and put it inside her *Jamborong*.

"Is your home near this area?" I asked.

"No, this side... around two kilometres away from here." She pointed her finger.

A few seconds later, I saw a woman carrying a plastic bag coming towards the shop. She was followed by a man walking in a swaying motion like he was pulled and pushed by that woman. He was shouting and rebuking her. Suddenly, it grasped my attention as I often got to see such incidents in my childhood days. People usually went to the weekly market via the road which was near our home. In the evening, when some people returned from the market and moved back to their homes, I often got to see such situations. Sometimes they sang old Bollywood songs loudly and spoke broken English throughout the road. The market was around five kilometres away from our home. It was the only market where my parents could dispose of the products we had. We didn't have any other alternative market in which my parents could sell arum, brinjal, chilli, ladies finger, bitter guard etc. Therefore, the prices were quite low. Sometimes, I went to that market with my parents, sat with them and waited for the customers like that boy sitting with his mother. One corner of the market was often filled with drinkers. Local people sold homemade rice beer; *Horlang* and *Hor Arak*. Apart from the rice beer, they also sold mixed chana, fried chicken, roasted pork and fried fish. These items used to be eaten with *Horlang* and *Hor Arak*. Again, another corner was often filled with dice gambling. Even though I couldn't understand anything, yet I used to peep when the players thronged into the throwing dice. I could only hear *jhandi, munda, lalpan, kalapan, chiriya, ita* and so on.

"That man is drunk," I said.

"Yes, he is. They are my neighbour; his wife is coming here to sell something. He is addicted to alcohol." She replied.

The woman looked too expressive and talkative. When I asked a question, she replied more than necessary. She wanted to roll her tongue continuously. Usually, when I get to talk with such people, I cut my words short and try to stay numb so that I can avoid some unnecessary conversations.

"They always fight at home. The man is a dipsomaniac, anyhow he tries to manage drinks. He always looks for ritual celebrations, social programmes and so on in villages so that he can wet his thirsty tongue with alcoholic drinks. His whole body shivers because of excessive consumption. Perhaps, he is now asking money from his wife." She started to roll her tongue again.

When she was speaking, I just nodded my head. I couldn't deviate from the track while she was in motion to express her words. I thought if she had been educated in formal education, she could have been a good storyteller and a good debater.

"Then, probably he cannot stay without alcohol." I grasped a second amidst her floating words.

"Yes, maybe. It seems his veins are carrying alcohol instead of blood. His body becomes a little yellowish and swollen. It reminds my past when I look at him." She said with a little sadness.

As I was a stranger to her, I didn't lend my interest while she was speaking. But when she did relate her story to him, my ears woke up. I thought she wanted to express the sadness that was stored for a long.

The drizzling rain was lessening; therefore, I could keep my head outside the ramshackle tin roof.

"Your husband......." I was trying to know about her husband.

"Yes, my husband. He passed away last year due to excessive consumption of alcohol. The same situation I have seen in them. Almost every day I was beaten ever since he started to drink alcohol." She woefully said about herself.

I was taken aback because an unknown lady was telling her story to an unknown traveller. I did not want to listen more as she became emotional.

"Now, how do you manage your expenses?" I tried to change the topic.

"Somehow I manage. I go to sell vegetables to our nearby weekly market, buy other things like pulses, potato, soap, cosmetics items at wholesale price and resale them in different villages." She replied with a little eagerness.

"You should be appreciated." I praised her.

"I am doing these works for my children's education, for their health, and for our daily needs. I do not do any illicit work, yet I heard some people try to mispresent my character. They do not understand the plight I have been facing." She sadly expressed.

I was shocked when she expressed her problem. I just nodded my head. When she finished her words, the lady who was carrying a plastic bag arrived there. Her drunk husband fell beside the road, probably because he could not maintain his physical balance.

"Where is your home?" She asked when I was ready to get inside my car.

"Rongkim," I replied.

While I was coming back and driving at average speed, I was thinking about the woman who was struggling to finance her children's education and dreamt of seeing her children successful one day. I was also thinking about that part of the society who tried to misshape her character.

www.ingramcontent.com/pod-product-compliance
Lightning Source LLC
LaVergne TN
LVHW041124150826
845673LV00007B/2177

* 9 7 9 8 8 9 3 2 2 5 6 4 8 *